the SOUTHERN NIGHTS Series

M. NEVER

The Southern Nights Series
Copyright © M. Never 2017
All rights reserved.

Names, characters and incidents depicted in this book are products of the author's imagination, or are used fictitiously. Any resemblance to actual events, locales, organizations, or persons, living or dead, is entirely coincidental and beyond the intent of the author or the publisher.

No part of this book may be reproduced or shared by any electronic or mechanical means, including but not limited to printing, file sharing, and email, without prior written permission from author.

Cover Design by:
Marisa Shor, Cover Me, Darling

Cover photo by:
Golden Czermak, FuriousFotog

Cover Model:
Justin White

Interior Design & Formatting by:
Christine Borgford, Type A Formatting

Editing by:
enny Sims, Editing4Indies, and Candice Royer

Proofread by:
Elaine York, Allusion Graphics, LLC/Publishing & Book Formatting

ONE SOUTHERN NIGHT

Kamdyn Ellis is the man.

Mr. All-Star athlete and resident bad boy . . . #7 quarterback on the field, and #1 player off.

Every guy at school wants to be him, and every girl at school wants to date him. Well, except Laney Summers, that is. The sassy city girl is the only one immune to Kam's clear blue eyes and arsenal of southern charm. But when a debilitating injury sidelines Kam's future and ability to play football, it's Laney who is tasked to be his tutor while he recuperates at home.

The chemistry between Kam and Laney is undeniable, and after months of ignoring what's clearly evident, Laney gives in. Allowing herself one night with Kam, no strings attached, no commitment to speak of. Alone, under the stars, on the fifty-yard line, Kam and Laney set out to discover if what they have is real, or just one steamy, southern night.

PROLOGUE

LANEY

THE CHEERLEADERS ON THE sidelines chant: Wolverines . . . let's hear you yell . . . blue . . . BLUE! Wolverines . . . let's hear you yell . . . white . . . WHITE! Put it together what's that spell . . . blue . . . white. The crowd echoes BLUE! WHITE! Then a cheerleader flies twenty feet in the air, touches her toes, and plummets back down to earth.

This weird phenomenon has become my life. Three months ago I couldn't fathom spending a Friday night in the stands of a stadium watching a football game. Yet, here I sit—in the middle of Nowhere, Alabama—cheering on the Wolverines in the state championships. Nowhere is where my father's from, and after my parents' divorce, he decided we needed to move out of New York City for a while. Which brings us to the here and now. Please don't get me wrong. I'm not opposed to football, but relocating to the Heart of Dixie has definitely opened my eyes to the magnitude, commitment, and love of the game in the South. My father has always been a diehard fan, but he's become a different man living here. In New York, celebrity Chef Riley (that's my dad) was going all the time. If not social networking on his phone, he was on the computer—if not the computer, he was in the kitchen cooking up new recipes. There wasn't much time to sit back and watch four quarters. When we moved, that all changed. Lately he seems to eat, sleep, and breathe the sport, much like everyone else in this small counrty town. I don't really get it. I do like the cheerleaders. My cousin, Miranda (the one who was flying through the air a minute ago), is co-captain. And honestly, if it wasn't for her, I'm not sure how the transition from big city to small town would have gone down.

It's been tolerable, so far. Especially when you get to ogle your chem partner every morning in first period. Said chem partner is also the quarterback currently kicking the other team's ass. Just like he said he was going to do. *Such the ego.*

The first day I met Kamdyn Ellis he called me sugar, and I nearly knocked him out. I informed him I have a name, and he had better use it. He laughed at me and then corrected himself, calling me Lemon, instead. Because as sweet as I look, I'm totally sour. I'm fine with him thinking that. I'm not interested in his arsenal of southern charm, boyish good looks, or baby blue eyes.

Hey, I said I'm not interested, not dead. He's hard not to notice. Especially when he's sitting a foot and a half away from you, wearing low slung jeans, a tight Roll Tide t-shirt, and backwards baseball cap.

See, not only have I noticed his southern charm, boyish good looks, and baby blue eyes, I've also noticed the revolving door of women he has on his arm. Like, a new one every other week. Sorry, I'm no one's hot and sweaty, solo, southern night.

So I keep my distance and flirt from afar, leaving him to his womanizing ways. Flirting with Kam has become one of the highlights of my day. Because, trust me when I tell you, living in Nowhere, Alabama, I need to be creative with my time.

KAM

I ZIP MY FLY.

Ahhhh. Nothing like a little stress reliever the morning of a big game. I help Darla stand. She runs her hands up my chest and locks her arms around my neck. "I love starting my day with you." She has that starry look in her pretty green eyes.

"Sugar, I'm a better caffeine rush than coffee." I smile, unhooking her hands.

"You're more than just a rush, Kam." She blinks up at me flirtatiously. "How about I wear your practice jersey to the game tonight, so I can show everyone I'm your number one fan."

Time out.

If there's one thing that screams 'item' in this school, it's wearing a player's football jersey. And, umm, no thanks. I'm not in the market for being anyone's significant other, boyfriend, or one half of an item. And Darla knows that. Everyone knows that. I spent the last three years with the most cold-hearted bitch in school, and I'm done with duos.

I'm done with status and done with image. Done with the captain of the football team dating the head cheerleader.

Senior year is all mine. No strings attached.

The warning bell rings for first period. Couldn't be better timing.

"We better go." I avoid responding altogether, making a quick getaway. Am I being a dick? Yeah, a little. But you shouldn't ask questions you already know the answer to. I open the door to the storage closet and peek my head out. The coast is clear, no faculty in sight. Get caught making out—or, in my case, getting head—and it's suspension row for us. I don't think The Touchdown Club would be too happy their star player had to ride the bench because he couldn't keep it in his pants.

Darla and I slip into the growing mass of students filling the hall. I move fast, snaking my way through my peers and away from Darla. Scot-free. Or so I think. I'm not ten feet in when I run smack dab into Laney Summers. She gives me that look. Her big blue eyes sharp. Yup, busted. She always knows.

"Blowin' off a little steam this morning?" she asks. Her tone is curt but amused at the same time. The city girl sometimes drops the G off her words. It's cute as hell. *She's cute as hell.*

"You know me so well." I smile down at her. The sweetest, most enticing smile I can manage. She rolls her eyes as we walk down the hallway and into chemistry together. The first time I met Laney was in this very spot. Chemistry class, the beginning of the school year. Our seats were already assigned, and lucky me, I got to sit with the new girl from New York, whom I knew all about already. Her cousin, Miranda, filled me in. Miranda was one of my ex's best friends until we broke up. Our separation divided our group, and Cheyenne actually demanded people choose sides. So everyone did, and they chose mine.

Laney was forced to move to Alabama when her parents got divorced. Pretty harsh moving the summer of your senior year. Miranda basically threatened my life if I wasn't nice to her. Me? Not nice? To a girl? I asked if she remembered whom she was talking to. What I wasn't prepared for was Laney not being nice to me! I called her sugar—not even thinking—I call everyone sugar. She snapped at me right off, saying she had a name and I better use it. I apologized and told her I'd use her name. From that moment on she's been Lemon. Sweet if you add sugar, sour if you don't, and I'm waiting for the moment I get to pour some sugar on her and really take a bite.

Sassy, city bitch.

I fell in love with her immediately.

"You coming to see me kick North's ass tonight?"

"You sound pretty confident in yourself, country boy." She drops her backpack on the floor next to the table covered with glass beakers, test tubes, and burners.

"I *am* confident, Lemon. We've beat them once already. Actually, I wouldn't even use the word beat, annihilated is more like it. It's in the bag. Bet I don't even get sacked." I cross my arms haughtily.

"Oh, well, if that's the case, I'll probably just stay home and surf Facebook. Doesn't sound like it's going to be a very interesting game." She curls her lip.

"Lemon," I stress, causing Laney to smile smugly. "Are you messing with me?"

"It's so easily done."

That's what she thinks.

"So, you are coming?" I sit down in my usual first period seat, with Laney a few inches away from me. It's my favorite place to be. Breathing in her . . . *exotic* scent. It's the only word I can come up with.

"Miranda would decapitate me if I didn't."

"Do you hate football so much that Miranda has to threaten you to go to a game?" The concept is foreign to me.

"No." She shrugs. "I just don't get what the big deal is. It's a game."

My mouth drops open. "Sugar, it's not just a game in these parts. It's a religion."

"Is that why there's a play called a Hail Mary?"

Now I'm the one rolling my eyes. "You don't like anything about football?"

She smirks darkly. "I like you in those tight pants."

My blood heats. "So, you do like me?"

"I like to look at you." She flirts. I love when Laney toys with me. It electrifies my insides.

"Lemon—" I lean in close to her ear, getting an injection of her intoxicating scent. "If you hang out with me after the game, I'll let you do so much more than just look."

She burns me with those scorching blue eyes. "Thanks, but no thanks. I'm not interested in being just another touchdown in your end zone."

I can't stop the ridiculous smile from spreading across my face. "I love when you talk dirty to me."

Actually, I love everything about Laney, from the way she looks with those red streaks running through her hair, to her casual Converse, and smart mouth. She's the anti-southern belle. And exactly what I need.

"You better be careful, Laney Summers, or else you might get caught from behind."

"Is that a threat, Kamdyn Ellis?"

I glare at her like I want to devour her. "It's a threat, and a promise, and a pledge."

"You don't scare me." She crosses her arms and scowls adorably.

"Oh, no? Care to put your money where your mouth is?"

"And what did you have in mind?" Her pretty eyes narrow.

"A bet of sorts."

"We're eighteen. We're not old enough to gamble."

"Then let's just keep it between us." I lower my voice provocatively.

"I'm listening."

"If we win tonight, I get you."

"Excuse me?" Laney's eyebrows shoot up.

"If we win the state championship, I get to have you, in the bed of my pickup, to do with what I want."

"You want me to bet my body?"

Maybe your heart, too? I hold back.

"It seems to be the only way you'll give me the time of day," I offer vulnerably, hoping my humble tone and baby blues will persuade her. It works on all the other girls, but Laney is different. She doesn't topple that easily. She needs persuading and a challenge.

She sighs, as if considering. "What's the spread?"

"Spread?"

"Yeah, you know, how much do you have to win by?"

"For a girl who claims she doesn't like football, you can talk a good game."

She shrugs. "It's discussed nonstop in my house. I listen with one ear open."

She is always surprising me. Since day one.

"Okay." I mull it over carefully; the last time we played North we won by seventeen and that was with all their starters healthy. Since then, they've lost two of their best players to injury: their quarterback and a tight end. "Twenty-point spread."

Laney's eyes widen. "That's a huge number. Are you that confident?"

"Baby." I put my hand on her leg and run it up her thigh. "Football is what I know. So, yes, you'll be mine tonight."

Chapter TWO

THE ROAR OF THE crowd is deafening. The smell of fresh cut grass intoxicating. The feel of the ball in my hands exhilarating.

I thrive on all of it. It's what causes my heart to beat and blood to flow through my veins. It's my vitality. I have lived football for as long I can remember. My mother says I was born to play. She knew the instant I threw my binky across the room at three months old. She's always said I was special, and I have always believed her. When I was a freshman, *Sports Illustrated* did a top ten article on football prodigies in the US, and I was number one. My whole life I have been compared to the likes of Tiger Woods and LeBron James. Descriptions like speed, power, and pinpoint accuracy have followed me everywhere. I've trained at the best football camps in the US with the most well-known names in the NFL. I broke the record for most passing attempts, most completions, and most passing yards my sophomore year. And have continued to crush those numbers into the ground. I was recruited by over fifty colleges and given full rides to all of them. Football is not only my future, it's my life. I dominate in the arena, and not a soul can touch me.

The cheerleaders are shouting on the sidelines and the announcer's voice is echoing into the clear night sky. I glance at the score board. Wolverines 35; Visitor 10. I told Laney we would spank them. Looks like I won that bet, and I fully intend to collect. But right now, I have to keep my head in the game and not think of Laney naked under the stars. Just the way I've always wanted her.

There's forty-five seconds left. This is the last pass of my high school career. It has to be legendary, not just for me, but for my brothers-in-arms. These ten guys have looked to me the last four years to lead them, and in doing so they have protected me, bled with me, and allowed me to thrive.

I call the play in the huddle: Gun south right, X flash on two.
Break!

We take formation up on the thirty-yard line. My center, Bugger, crouches down. He's an as-big-as-life black dude, snarling at the opposing team. I take one last look around the stadium. This is the start and the end of my legacy. Miranda flies twenty feet in the air as the cheerleaders below her chant blue and white. The clock feels like it's ticking down in slow motion, and the monstrous defensive lineman, who's had my number all night, looks like he wants to rip my head off. It's a collective adrenaline rush.

"I'm coming for you, Q," number sixty-seven growls.

"You'll have to get through me first," Bugger rumbles, and I just smile. "Might as well go home. We wiped your ass with the field. *Again.*"

Sixty-seven howls. The guy actually howls like a freakin' injured coyote.

It's time to finish this.

"Blue forty-two!" I scream out. "Blue forty-two! Hike! Hike!" Bugger snaps the ball right into my hands, a perfect exchange, and everyone disperses in a frenzy. The lines collide like Spartans going to war as I scan the field for my receiver. I watch Duece burn grass down the center and everything inside me ignites. It's the same feeling every time. A tingly sensation under my skin, like pins and needles. This, right here, this second, is pure control. An untouchable feeling. I see my opening and take it, firing the ball down range. A perfect spiral headed straight for the end zone. I watch it spin and land right into Duce's hands. The crowd explodes. "*TOUCHDOWN, Wolverines!*" the announcer yells, "*And new Alabama State Champions!*"

I break out in goose bumps right before everything goes black.

Sack!

Chapter THREE

I BLINK MY EYES. They feel heavy.

I look around trying to figure out where I am. There's muted, flourescent lights and a bleachy smell. I try to move, but my limbs feel like lead.

I groan, and it vibrates roughly through my whole body. *Where am I? What's happening?*

"Well, good morning," a pleasant voice chirps from above me. A woman I don't recognize comes into my eye-line. My heart palpitates, and I hear quick beeping in the room. "It's okay, Mr. Ellis, you're fine." The older woman with kind brown eyes tries to soothe me.

"Where am I?" I croak. What the fuck is wrong with my voice?

"You're at County State Hospital, darlin.'" She fluffs up my pillow.

Hospital?

"What happened?" I can barely push the words out.

She pours me some water. "Here, drink this. Your mouth is dry." The water is cold and quenches my thirst. It feels like I've been sleeping in the desert. "I'm going to get the doctor and your mama."

"What happened?" I ask again, but she doesn't provide me with a response.

"Just hold tight. They'll explain everything, sugar."

"KAM!" A FEW MINUTES after the nurse disappears, my mother rushes to my side. "Baby, we were so worried." She kisses me all over my face.

"What happened?" I ask for what feels like the hundredth time.

"Baby, you had an accident of sorts. During the game, you were sacked after your last pass. It was a cheap shot by the other team. Something happened in your brain when you got hit. The doctor can explain it better. But you didn't get up." Tears pool in her distressed, hazel eyes. "I thought we lost you."

"My brain?" I repeat, my voice becoming a little stronger.

"Yeah, baby. You had surgery. You've been in a coma for two weeks."

"Two weeks?"

She nods, the tears falling down her cheeks. A moment later, an older man with a white coat and glasses enters the room holding a tablet.

"Mr. Ellis." He attempts a smile, which doesn't really work for him. "Welcome back."

"Where the hell did I go?"

"First, I'm Dr. Saltzman." He puts his hand out. I lift my arm with some difficulty and we shake. He seems to be assessing my every move. "I performed your surgery and have been monitoring your progress." He pulls a chair up to the side of my bed and takes a seat. *Make yourself at home, why don't you.* "Mr. Ellis, you had a brain aneurysm, or cerebral hemorrhage, during the game. I suspect it was always there, but when you were hit, it ruptured, causing a bleed in your brain."

All I can do is blink as I process the words aneurysm, cerebral, and hemorrhage.

"We repaired what needed to be fixed, but you didn't come out of the coma right away. This is sometimes normal."

"Am I okay?" I glance at my mother restlessly.

"Yes, as far as I can see. We'll have to do some more scans now that you're awake, and you'll have to stay in the hospital for observation for a few weeks, but I think you are going to recover just fine."

"So I can still play football?"

"As long as there are no stemming neurological effects."

"Neurological effects?" Too many medical terms I don't like in one conversation.

"We don't know the extent of the damage the hemorrhage caused, if any. We'll know more as you recuperate. You'll need physical therapy to reverse the muscle weakness from the coma."

"Is that why I can barely lift my arm, Doc?" I make a fist.

"Yes."

"How long?"

"How long what, Mr. Ellis?"

"How long will it take me to recover?" I press.

"Well, that depends on you, and how your body responds to the therapy. In my opinion, you are in exceptional shape—young, athletic. You should have no issues bouncing back as long as you are committed to therapy."

I glance at my mom again. She's been silent the whole time but looks like she's ready to fall apart.

"When can I start?" I ask Dr. Saltzman.

He tries to smile again. His thin lips look like a squiggly line. A happy face really doesn't work for this man.

"We'll get you up and walking in a little while. You'll start physical therapy here in the hospital while under observation. I'm going to recommend you stay at home for a month or so after you are released, so you can solely concentrate on rehab. I think a stress-free environment will aid in the recovery process."

"I'm good with that." I'm confident, ready to face this head on.

Dr. Saltzman nods, then stands.

"Thank you." I track him with my eyes gratefully.

"It's what I'm here for. Now, hurry up and get better. The Crimson Tide needs a quarterback next year." He winks.

I can't help but snicker. Everyone's a fan, even straight-edged neurosurgeons with the quirky smile.

"Mom, you okay?" I turn my attention to my mother once Dr. Saltzman leaves. She nods, but the dam breaks.

"I'm sorry, Kam. I want to be strong." She wipes her eyes. "But, baby, almost losing you . . ."

"Mom, stop." I can't stand it when she cries. "Just come here and hug me." I can't stand it when any girl cries. She darts the two feet separating us and gingerly wraps her arms around me, her tears wetting my cheek. I hold onto her as much as my weak muscles will allow. This really sucks. I feel helpless. "You heard the doctor. I'm going to be okay." I try to reassure her.

"I know, thank God." She pulls away from me and smiles rubbing her swollen eyes and red nose.

"That will be it, baby, I promise. No more tears. Unless they're of joy. You're awake and alive, and that's something to celebrate."

"Damn straight." I try to sound cheerful, but I'm suddenly really, really tired.

"Dad is picking up Trevor and Luke from school. They should be here in a little bit. He was upset he left right before you woke up."

"How's he doing?" My parents divorced when I was ten and my twin brothers were six. He still plays a very active role in our lives, despite being remarried and living in another town.

"He's a mess. His all-star, golden boy and first-born son? He would be done if he lost you. We both would."

"Well, apparently it's kind of hard to get rid of me."

"And we thank our lucky stars for that." She kisses my head. "Get some rest so your brothers can come and harass you."

"Can't wait." I yawn, barely able to keep my eyes open.

PHYSICAL THERAPY IS A mind fuck.

My brain says run, but my body laughs and holds me hostage at a snail's pace on the treadmill. It's been three weeks since I woke up from the coma. Two weeks were spent in the hospital and the last week I've spent at home, focusing on rehab. I didn't realize the toll being unconscious for fourteen days took on my body until I tried to stand. It's like everything just stopped working and has been protesting to start up again ever since.

"Come on, Kam, two more minutes, then you're done," my trainer, Dylan, says. He's been assigned my case. That's what I'm called, *a case*. It pisses me off royally. I'm Kamdyn Fucking Ellis, not *a case*. Not an invalid or some impaired Joe Schmo, even though that's how I feel at the moment.

"Just rev it and give my body a challenge. I'm tired of the leisurely strolls." I bark, frustrated.

Dylan laughs, his big, brown eyes sparkling. He doesn't look much older than me, even though he claims to be in his mid-twenties. "Look, all-star. I get you're used to pushing your body. But it's still recovering. I'm not going to chance an injury just because your inner warrior wants a battle. For now, you just have to grin and bear it. We'll get there."

"Grrrr . . ." I can't stand this. "I want to run, I want to punch, kick, shred. I feel like a walking set of stripped bones."

"Easy, killer." Dylan laughs mild mannerly. He's like the most laid-back person I've ever met. It's annoying, frankly.

The treadmill beeps and turns off. I am beyond frustrated. I hate this. I want to be better. *Tomorrow*. "I know this is hard on you, seeing as you've probably never been held back a day in your life." So true. "It's an emotional challenge as much as a physical one. You just have to stay in the zone and keep your eye on the ball." Dylan places a hand on my shoulder.

I grimace. Laney's football references are so much sexier.

I've been thinking about her a lot lately. I miss our back and forth banter in chem and hearing her laugh, and seeing her smile. Is that crazy? Maybe. But she's definitely someone I like to be around. And being sequestered has made me realize that. A highlight of mine was when I received a card from her while I was in the hospital. It read:

An apple a day keeps the doctor away . . . If you have good aim and it's accurate.

Kam, this card made me think of you. Hope you get well soon. Chem sucks without you.

Laney xo

I contemplated calling her but decided against it. What would I say? Hey, want to come over and hang out with a cripple who may never play football again? Whose future might be fucked? Yeah. I don't think so. Who'd want to spend time with a loser like that?

I step off the treadmill, my body a pathetic sack.

"Good work today." Dylan slaps me on the back. I want to growl at him, but I don't. I'm going to beat this recovery into the ground then run ten miles over it.

I slip into my mother's 4Runner and stare mindlessly out the window as she drives away from the rehab center.

"There's someone coming from school tonight to start tutoring you while you're home," she reminds me.

"I didn't forget." I roll my eyes. I can't wait to see who the school designated for this. Probably some nerd from the academics team who's going to put me back in a coma. My life is *so* great.

"Good. I'm making spaghetti and meatballs for dinner tonight," she nudges me, as if trying to cheer me up.

"I'd rather have homemade mac and cheese." I give her the puppy dog eyes.

She glances over and smiles a surrendering expression. My mother can never say no to me when I'm sick. Even if those times have been few and far between. I think my last devastating illness was freshman year when I had the flu, and all I wanted to eat was watermelon. So weird.

"Fine. I'll drop you off then go to the store. Spoiled."

"You made me that way."

She smirks. "Sometimes you deserve it."

Chapter FOUR

I HOBBLE UP THE stairs.

My mother hovers in the foyer until I make it to the top. "I'm fine," I gripe.

"I know," she responds. "Just playing it safe."

"Playing it safe gets you nowhere."

I hear her sigh. It's an amused sound. "I'll be back in a little bit. The door is open for the tutor."

I throw my hand up over my head in acknowledgement. Tutor. *Yay.*

I drop down onto my bed. The fun starts soon. I'm going to try and enjoy my last shred of peace and quiet before I am officially tortured by some scrawny dork quizzing me on *Beowulf* and international politics.

The doorbell rings abruptly. Here we go. "Come in!" I yell, right after I consider smothering myself with a pillow.

I hear someone walk up the stairs. "Kam?" a girl's voice carries down the hall. *Oh, shit.*

"In here."

A few seconds later, Darla walks into my room. *Double shit.*

"Hey," she drawls with a sugary smile.

"Hey," I respond flatly. I need this like I need a hole in my head. Ever since I got out of the hospital she's been texting me nonstop. Asking how I am and if I need anything. I tried to be polite and tell her I was fine, and not to worry over me, but that is just not happening. "What are you doing here?"

Please, don't be my tutor. Dear God, please.

"I just wanted to see you. Been missing you, that's all." She walks into my room warily, like she isn't sure if she should be here.

She shouldn't.

"Oh, yeah? Sorry about that. Been a bit preoccupied recovering and all." I motion to my worthless limbs.

"Well, I thought I could make it a little less painful for you." She saunters toward my bed.

"Darlin', the only thing that's going make it less painful is if I go back in time."

Darla frowns. Her blonde hair is curled, perfect ringlets framing her face, and dressed exactly like my bitchy ex. Pristine. An image to be had.

"Well, I can't turn back time, but history can definitely repeat itself, if you want." She crawls onto the bed like a cat stalking a mouse. I just lie there and watch her move, coming closer and closer to my weary body. I contemplate so many things in that moment. Should I let her touch me? Should I send her away? My body is screaming for the release, but my head wants no part of the aftermath. She wants more. It's evident. And I just don't, at least not with her. She's too much of the same, too much of what appalls me.

Darla reaches me and begins kissing my neck. My body and my mind wage war. I shouldn't let her do this, but Jesus Christ, I need it so bad. My eyes roll to the back of my head as she works her mouth over my skin. My body responds, but my brain shuts down. "Darla." I grab her arms, stopping her.

"Kam?" She looks back at me, confused.

"Please, stop." I clench my jaw.

"What?" Her eyes widen.

"I can't do this."

"Can't do what? Fool around? Your part's broken or something?"

I glare at her. "No, it works just fine. I'm just not that into you anymore." I finally break the news.

Her green eyes darken with rage. "The tent in your pants says otherwise," she snaps.

"Yeah, well, that head isn't in charge at the moment. I've tried to be nice, but you're just not getting the message. I don't want to see you anymore."

She rears back with a hurt expression on her face. Fuck. This is never easy. *Why do they get so attached?* I'm always honest up front. Shit, I couldn't be any clearer if I wore a sign. *No relationships. Just fun.*

Someone suddenly coughs in the doorway. I look past Darla and gape. "Lemon?" I sit up straighter.

"Is this a bad time?" Laney measures me and Darla in the very compromising position on my bed.

"Not at all," I immediately answer. Darla pins me with her eyes. "What are you doing here?"

"I'm here to study." She holds up a very full backpack.

"You're my tutor?"

"Uh-huh," she responds. I think I hear angels singing. "I'll come back though . . ."

"No! Darla was just leaving." I all but launch her off me.

"You sure about that?" Laney asks snidely, and goosebumps rise on my arms. Shit, I missed that smart mouth.

"Yes." I look pointedly at Darla. She pouts, but there's fire in her eyes. I don't like it one bit.

"Yeah, I was just leaving." Darla slinks off my bed. She smooths out her skirt, lifts her chin, before starting for the door. She walks past

Laney without so much as a hello, and it pisses me off to no end. Most of the girls in school think it's okay to brush her off because she isn't like them. A Stepford southern belle with a pole stuck up her ass. "Kam, you know my number. Call me when you feel better," Darla tosses over her shoulder right before she leaves.

Um, yeah. Darla. *Delete.*

After she's gone, it's just me and Laney and a whole room of awkward silence. I break the ice.

"Hi."

I never said it was going to be with poetry or anything.

"Hi," Laney responds with an entertained smile. I know what she's thinking. Once a player, always a player. I wish she knew how wrong she was. Laney strolls into my room and drops the book bag by my desk, then takes a look around. I love her confidence and comfort in her own skin. She isn't intimidated by all the trophies or the black and white pictures of me playing hanging on the wall. Captured movements suspended in time. My favorite is the close-up where I'm just about to fire the football into the end zone. It's a representation of my dream, of my focus, of my life. It's also a reminder those things might all be gone.

"It's sort of just how I pictured it." She crosses her arms over her chest.

"And how is that?" I question.

"All jock."

"It's not all jock." I dispute. "I still have Mr. Wiggles." I hold up a small, brown bear I've had for as long as I can remember. I never could let go of this stupid stuffed animal.

"Oh, well, that makes it much less masculine then." Laney sits down in the chair at the desk. Somehow she fits. "Ready to get started?"

"Meh."

"Senioritis kicking in?" She pulls out a few, thick, hardcover books.

"I guess."

"I promise I'll make it as painless as possible."

With you here, I feel no pain at all.

"Sounds like a plan. How did you get slated for the job anyway?" I take the notebook she hands me.

"I was in the office when Principal Adams was talking to Julius Maxwell. He was your original tutor."

"Orange Julius?" I curl my lip. Biggest brain at school. We call him Orange Julius because of his crazy, ginger hair and freckles. He also talks like he's whining. All. The. Time. My skin crawls just thinking about it.

"Yup. He looked like he wanted to throw up. I don't think he liked the idea of being your tutor."

"That's probably because I used to give him wedgies and shove him in his locker freshman year. I've grown up since then, but he still avoids me like the plague."

"Geez, I don't blame him." Laney grimaces at me.

"I'm not that guy anymore," I argue petulantly.

"You sure?" she toys with me.

"*Yesss*," I cross my arms. "So, how did you end up my tutor anyway?" I'm completely invested in the story now.

Laney looks guilty as she fiddles with the pen she's holding. "I sort of stepped in."

"Stepped in how?"

"I felt bad for Julius. He looked so uncomfortable. So, I told Principal Adams that I was your chem partner and was worried about my grade. And maybe it would be better if I was your tutor so we could stay on the same page."

"And he bought that?"

"Yeah, Julius couldn't bow out fast enough." She giggles freely. Man, did I miss that sound.

"So, now you have to put up with me?"

Laney shrugs. "As long as you don't try to give me a wedgie, things should be fine."

I laugh. I may not give her a wedgie, but I will definitely try to get as close to her underwear as possible. Ideally, pulling them off with my teeth.

"I'm not making any promises," I joke.

"I wouldn't expect you to. I know your M.O." She eyes me judgmentally.

Ouch.

"Let's just get to studying," I suggest. I don't want her running for the hills before we even get started.

"It's what I'm here for. Start with history?" She sits back down in the chair at my desk and folds her feet under her legs Indian-style. She looks so cute sitting there, in my room, even though I wish she was in my bed. I shake the thought off—I can keep dreaming. If Laney wanted no part of me before, it couldn't help my case that she found Darla pawing all over me earlier.

"Let's read the chapter and do the review questions at the end. That's the request from most of your teachers. I'm supposed to bring tests to you on Friday. But according to the notes, they can be open book. You sure have the life," she quips.

"What is that supposed to mean?" I ask defensively.

"Nothing. You're big man on campus and definitely treated as such." Laney flips open her history book.

"It's not my fault I'm good at football."

"I never said there was anything wrong with being a good athlete. But you can't deny you get the royal treatment." She defends her statement.

I sigh. "I can't change that. It is what it is." Unless I never play football again. And then my future, and my life, is fucked. "Weren't there people in your old high school who were popular? Who got to slide on things?"

"Sure, there were." She smirks, still looking down at her book.

"And it didn't bother you?"

Laney's smile gets bigger.

"What am I missing, Lemon?"

She looks up at me with just her eyes. "It was me. I was treated just like you."

"You?"

"My father is a celebrity chef. In New York that's a big deal."

"You're a total hypocrite." I accuse.

"I know. But you're fun to play with."

"You have no idea how much fun I can be." I insinuate.

"You're right, I'm deprived. I guess I'm a masochist."

I shake my head. She drives me nuts. And I love it. "Let's just get to studying."

"Way ahead of you." She flips a page.

Laney and I read in silence. It's a chapter on the Korean War, but I'm barely retaining a word. All my attention is focused on the hot brunette sitting across from me, wearing faded jeans that hug her body and a top that resembles a baseball player's warm-up jersey. I wonder if she wore it on purpose. The shirt's grey and black with the number fourteen stamped on her chest. I keep glancing at it, wishing it was the number seven. *My number.*

"Done yet?" Laney looks up and catches me staring.

"Yup." I smile, trying to cover.

"Good. Let's answer the study guide questions then compare notes."

"Sounds good." I agree.

Laney picks up her pen and starts writing while I just stare at the notebook in front of me. Grabbing my pen, holding it awkwardly between my fingers, I read the first question silently. *Why did North Korea cross the 38th Parallel and invade South Korea?*

I know the answer. Now I just have to get it onto the paper. I place the ball point tip of the pen on the blue line and attempt to write. *North Korea . . .* I'm not two words in when my hand starts to shake. The words become nothing but illegible scribbles. My heart hammers in my chest as I try harder and harder to control my hand. But it's no use. Control is the last thing I have. I throw the pen and notebook across the room.

"Fuck!"

Laney startles and looks up. "What wrong?"

"I hate the fucking Korean War," I erupt.

"What?" Her pretty blue eyes are confused.

I'm falling apart inside. Every time I try to do anything with my right hand, it ends with something either broken or thrown across the room. The one part of my body I need to work most is being the most difficult, and I'm reminded every damn day that my dreams are slipping away. And I just don't know how I'm going to handle it when the gauntlet drops and my life disintegrates. Five words will seal my fate: You can't play football anymore.

"Kam?" Laney is standing beside me now. How long has she been there? "You okay? You checked out for a second."

"I'm fine, Lemon. Sorry. I didn't mean to frighten you. Just this whole healing thing is a little frustrating sometimes."

I wonder if she's buying my bull.

"Frustrating?" she repeats, like she's testing the word. "I'd call it more maddening based on your earlier outburst."

Nope, not buying my BS for one second. Laney retrieves the notebook and pen from across the room. Watching her bend over makes me feel a little bit better.

Laney looks down at the pad, and I know I've stepped in shit now based on her facial expression. It's puzzled, and I think a little sad. She looks up at me with soft eyes. I have no idea what to say. I don't want to talk about it. I don't want face the truth if it's real.

Laney walks across the room, straight for me. I watch every soft step she takes. My blood heats up. It seems the closer she is to me, the warmer my insides become. And it's not just from arousal, she also excites my heart.

Laney makes no qualms about sitting next to me on the mattress. She positions my textbook in front of her and rests my notebook on her lap. Then she grabs my hand and places the pen between my fingers. I tense as she encloses her hand over mine, like how you'd teach a child how to trace. The feel of her skin is euphoric, and I'm at a loss to even come up with a word for the way she smells. I don't need one; I'm fine just getting high off the scent. It has my cells pumping right along with the rhythm of my pulse. Laney starts to move our connected hands like one.

"When I was a little girl," she begins, never looking away from the notebook, "I wouldn't eat anything but spaghetti. And, being the chef that he is, it drove my father crazy. But after a while, making spaghetti became our thing. He would hold my hand like this." She squeezes my fingers. "And teach me how to stir the sauce. I wasn't very good at it, at first. It took a lot of practice. I would flick it all over the stove. But the more spaghetti we made, the better I became at stirring the sauce."

Laney stops writing and I look down at the words we wrote together: Practice Makes Perfect.

Such a simple statement, and maybe before I would have believed it. But now? It seems hopeless.

"I'm not so sure, Lemon."

Laney glances at me, she's sitting a little bit in front of me so she has to turn her head slightly. The look in her eyes is sexy as hell.

"I am. You're Kamdyn Ellis, star quarterback, on and off the field."

"What if I never recover? What then? Who will I be then?" My throat tightens with emotion from just the mere thought.

She shrugs simply. "You'll have to figure that out."

"You make it sound so easy."

"It is and it isn't. I wondered the same thing when my father told me we were moving to Alabama. I thought my life was over. I was leaving everything I knew. My friends, my school, my boyfriend—"

"Boyfriend?" I interrupt. "You never told me you had a boyfriend."

"I don't. Not anymore. We broke up when I left."

"Sorry, " I offer, although I'm not really sorry at all.

"It's okay. It didn't really break my heart. He was nice, but it wasn't love."

"So, what, now you're stuck in Alabama totally miserable?"

"See, that's the thing. I thought I was going to be miserable, but I'm not. It's different. Don't get me wrong, I miss New York terribly, but the country is growing on me."

"I don't think I'd ever be able to get past not playing football." I look down at my hand, and squeeze it into a fist.

"You'll have to accept it just wasn't meant to be."

"I'm not a quitter," I argue, but there isn't much fight in my voice.

"I'm not saying you are. And I'm not saying you won't fully recover and go on to become a Heisman Trophy winner. I'm just saying that if that doesn't happen, there are other options. Don't box yourself in. You might find happiness in unexpected places."

"Are you happy, Lemon?" I ask genuinely.

Laney bats her eyelashes. "I'm getting there." I don't know why, but that statement makes me feel the first burst of hope in three weeks. I let go of the pen and turn my hand over, entwining her fingers tightly with mine. She analyzes the gesture.

"Kam—" she sighs.

"Laney," I cut her off, "I'm really glad it's you and not Orange Julius who's here."

She smirks at me but doesn't have a chance to respond as my mother chooses that moment to appear with dinner.

"Homemade mac and cheese like the patient requested." She halts when she walks into the room and sees me and Laney holding hands on my bed. "Hope I'm not interrupting something?" Oh, crap, she has that 'you're in trouble' tone.

"No, nothing." Laney springs up. "Kam was just having some trouble holding the pen. I was trying to help." She goes over and sits back down at the desk.

"Oh." My mother's face falls. Laney couldn't have spoken a more perfect sentence. She just got us off the hook big time. My mother knows how hard this recovery is for me. She's seen the depression take hold and try to drag me under. She isn't going to blow a little thing like hand holding out of proportion, especially if it preceded an issue with my control.

My mom places the tray of food on my bed then picks up the extra dish and glass of iced tea and serves Laney. "The deal was I would feed you dinner while you were here. It's not gourmet like you're probably used to, but I've never had any complaints."

Laney smiles up at my mom. "I'm sure it's amazing. And trust me, sometimes gourmet isn't all it's cracked up to be."

"Oh? Your daddy is a world-renowned chef. I can't imagine you've ever eaten a bad meal in your life."

"Bad? No. Weird, yes. He tried to put dandelions in the salad when I was twelve."

"Really?" I chime in. "That *is* weird."

"It's only the tip of the iceberg." Laney shakes her head and rolls her eyes.

"Well, you must have had a very educational upbringing. Probably nothing like the one we had."

"Do you know my father?"

"Mmmm-hmmm. Before he was a famous chef, he was just another guy trying to survive home ec." My mother laughs.

"You went to high school together?" Laney asks, surprised. "He didn't say anything to me when I told him I was tutoring Kam."

"He probably doesn't even remember me. He left right after graduation and never looked back." My mom's voice sounds sad. "Anyway, eat up. I don't want you getting home too late."

"Yes, ma'am." Laney grabs the bowl and scoops some shells into her mouth. "Wow. This is delicious."

My mom smiles. "I'll take that as the highest compliment, coming from you."

"I'll tell you what. I'll trade you dandelions for macaroni and cheese any day." Laney strikes a deal.

"Done."

"Thanks, Mom," I say as she leaves the room.

"Anything for you, dear," she drawls from the hallway, causing me to smile.

"Your mom is pretty cool," Laney comments as she munches away on her dinner.

"Yeah, she's the best. I don't know what I would do without her." I scoop some macaroni into my mouth with my left hand. It's so yum.

"You'd probably have to learn to do your own laundry," Laney remarks.

"You're so funny," I snark, "I'll never do my own laundry."

Laney snickers. "I believe you."

"Hope you know how to sort." I leer at her.

Laney pauses with the spoon by her lips, her mouth slightly open. "I'll never do your laundry, Kam."

"We better hire a housekeeper then."

"Keep dreaming, all-star." She smiles and then continues eating. *Cock-blocked every time.*

After a small conversation reprieve, I ask, "So, the country is finally growing on you?"

Laney shrugs. "I guess. I can appreciate the open landscape and living by the lake."

"The lake is definitely a bonus." I agree.

"I also like that my dad is happy."

"He wasn't in New York?"

"No. Toward the end of my parents' marriage, things were really bad. I'm probably the only kid in the world who breathed a sigh of relief when they told me they were getting a divorce. I just didn't know my father had plans of leaving the state once it was over."

"Where's your mom? Why didn't you stay with her?"

"What's today's date?" she muses, "I think she's in Bangkok. She travels a lot, like all the time. That's why I'm with my dad. He has full custody. All those spaghetti dinners? It was just the two of us."

"Do you get along with your mom? Even though you don't see her?" I don't know if I'm prying, and I'm sure Laney will let me know once I step over the line, but she seems comfortable enough talking about her mother, so I'm going to push it as far as she'll let me go.

"Yeah, actually, she's great. We talk all the time. I wish I saw her more." She stabs her spoon into the bowl a few times.

"Damn. I couldn't imagine not seeing my mom. I don't know what I'd do."

"I think we established you'd have to learn to do laundry."

"Smart-ass." I would fling some macaroni at her if I could.

"Yup." She twists the spoon in her mouth and drags it over her tongue. Damn. Her little gesture just made my dick twitch. "You ready to finish?"

"Finish?" I ask awkwardly. My pants now have a pulse.

"Yeah, with studying. You tell me the answers, and I'll write."

"How about you help me write?" *How about you just touch me, in general?*

Laney cocks an eyebrow at me.

"Come on. What happened to practice makes perfect? You can teach me how to stir the sauce."

"Oh, using my own words against me. Nice." She places her bowl down.

"I'm a competitor. What I can I say? I'll do anything to win."

"I bet." Laney relents, and comes and sits next to me. "No funny business. We're studying."

I make an X over my heart. "I solemnly swear I'm up to no good."

"At least you're honest." She grabs my hand, and my senses charge like electromagnetic energy. Her touch feels like the sun brightening a whole new day.

Maybe recovering isn't going to be so bad after all.

Chapter FIVE

I'M UP TO EIGHT mph on the treadmill.

It's been nearly two months, and my body has bounced back with a vengeance. I'm lifting close to what I was before the aneurysm and running almost as far and as long. I feel good. I feel energized, but I'm not out of the woods yet. And that's frustrating as hell.

"Nice job, Kam." Dylan brings my speed down to a brisk walk. I'm panting and sweaty.

"Thanks. That felt great," I huff. Dylan laughs his cool, nothing in the world bothers me, laugh.

"I wish more of my cases said that after a thirty-minute run."

"I'm not most cases." I remind him.

"No, you're definitely not. I'll be bragging about you for the rest of my life."

I roll my eyes. "Only brag if I end up becoming someone to brag about."

Dylan frowns. "Still having trouble with the coordination?"

I punch the off button and the treadmill dies. "Yes. I can write and eat now, but I still can't regain my accuracy. I picked up a football the other day and tossed it at the tire swing a few times. I could barely hit it, let alone get it through the hole."

"It will come," Dylan assures me. Glad he is so confident because I'm freaking out. Spending the last two months with Dylan nearly every day has built our relationship significantly. His laidback attitude annoyed me at first, but now I know it's just what I needed. When I was battling through reps I used to be able to do in my sleep and on the verge of a meltdown, Dylan kept me calm. He encouraged me, talked to me, and I soon understood the method to his madness. Although, he would argue it isn't madness, and that I'm the only crazy one in the room. Being on the verge of losing all your hopes and dreams can do that to a person.

"Yeah, well, it better come soon. The head coach from Alabama checks in on me once a week. And the fact that all I can tell him is 'I'm working hard, sir' isn't really sitting well. I'm afraid I'm going to lose my spot—*my chance.*"

"You're not going to lose anything. Sometimes recovery is as much mental as it is physical. You're in limbo right now. It will all come together, trust me. It's just going to take a little time."

"A little time is all I have."

"You know what you need?"

"No, do tell," I respond cynically.

"To have a little fun."

"Fun? I forgot what fun is."

"Exactly. You need to be reminded. Go out and do something new. Something you've never done before."

I raise my eyebrows at him. An image of Laney naked in my bed springs to mind. That would definitely be fun. But I know that's not what he means. There's not much to do in this small Alabama town besides off-roading, swimming in the lake, or hanging out at Sonic on a Saturday night.

"I'll work on it," I tell him, a picture of Laney completely bare still dominating my thoughts.

He smiles aloofly at me as I step off the treadmill. "Good."

I really want to ask him how much pot he smokes.

I wipe the sweat off my brow, clasp hands with Dylan and confirm my appointment for Monday. One more week and I'll be back at school. I can't wait and am apprehensive all at the same time. It's a really sucky place to be.

Once home, I wait for Laney like the puppy I've become, always anxious for her arrival. Spending the last two months with her has been the only thing making this recovery bearable. It's unbelievable how she can distract me from everything going on in my life. How she can make me forget I'm supposed to be Superman and just be satisfied being Clark Kent. No one has ever affected me like that before. And the more time we spend together, the more I want to tell her how she makes me feel. But every time I get the courage, she reminds me of our place. Strictly platonic. It doesn't matter that she laughs at my jokes or her eyes blaze whenever I touch her. She keeps a safe distance between us. She doesn't trust me, no matter how many hints I drop. And not just hints I want her physically. I want the total package—I want Laney to be my girlfriend. I didn't think I was ever going to want that again, not after Cheyenne and her manipulative, self-centered ways. But Laney is nothing like her. It doesn't matter to her that I'm some hometown celebrity put on a pedestal because I'm a football god. Or that I'm the Crimson Tide's starting quarterback next year. She's told me repeatedly football is just a game to her. She doesn't understand the hype, and that is sort of refreshing. Although, sometimes I want to shake her so she understands just what a big deal it is around here, what a big deal it is to *me*. She can drive me crazy like no other, and for some reason I love it.

I tried to kiss her last week. I couldn't even control myself, but she retreated so fast, the room teetered. Being around her is becoming harder and harder. I don't know what to do; I don't know how to break down the door. I'm close to saying fuck it, tying her up, and shouting in her face with a megaphone: *I like you! I want to be with you! I'm not going to hurt you! You're not like the others!*

I would actually do it, too, if I thought it would work.

I hear the doorbell. She's finally here and she's late. What's that about? Then I remember that volleyball tryouts were this afternoon. Who knew my little, surly, city girl was an athlete at heart? Makes me love her even more.

Laney comes bouncing into my room, her book bag slung over one shoulder and a pizza box in her hands.

"Hey." I smile brightly at her.

"Hey." She smiles back and drops her book bag onto the floor, never letting go of the pizza.

"How were tryouts?"

"Okay, I guess. We'll see next week. This picking the players over the weekend is killer."

"Yeah, I don't know why they do it that way. Stupid."

"Tell me about it," she agrees as she puts the box on my desk and takes a seat in her chair. Yes, her chair. I've dubbed it that since it's where she sits every night.

"What's with the food?" I ask with a chin thrust.

"I thought since it was Friday and you've been working so hard, we'd forgo studying and just hang out."

"Seriously?"

"Yup."

"You want to just hang out, with me, tonight?" I repeat, making sure I heard her correctly.

"Yes." She giggles. She's wearing that shirt again. The gray and black one with the number fourteen stamped across her chest. I don't think there's an article of clothing I find more appealing. Laney picks up her book bag and pulls out paper plates, napkins, and two bottles of soda. "I thought we'd give your mom the night off. My dad made the pizza for us."

"The famous Chef Riley cooked for me?" I sit up straighter on my bed.

"He was thrilled to do it. I think he wants your autograph," she informs me as she plates a piece of pizza for each of us. It smells out of this world. Laney hands me my slice. It's square, which is odd, and there're little circles of mozzarella all over the top of it.

"Kam, what's wrong, you look confused?" Laney asks as she sits next to me on the bed.

"I'm not used to pizza looking like this," I admit.

Laney nearly falls over laughing. "It's called a grandma pie, all fresh ingredients. My father made the mozzarella himself."

"He made the cheese? I can't even begin to imagine how you make cheese."

"It's a very involved process. Lots of kneading." She smirks. "And you don't ask Chef Riley to cook and expect store-bought ingredients."

"Well, I'll send him a signed football for his trouble."

"Thank you." She nibbles on her pizza.

"You know, you could have just asked me."

"Asked you what?" She plays dumb.

"For an autograph, if your dad wanted one."

"I didn't want to make you feel uncomfortable. Or make your ego any bigger than it already is." She grins all cutesy at me.

"You can ask me for anything, Lemon. I'll never say no."

"You spoil me," she jokes. I wish she knew how much I want to spoil her. Spend time with her, touch her, make her smile.

"I can be a pretty good boyfriend, if given the chance." Laney nearly chokes on her pizza, and I pat her back. "You okay?"

"Fine . . . that statement was just surprising."

"Why?"

"Because, there are plenty of girls at school who would die to be your girlfriend."

"Yeah, well I'm not interested in any of them." I contest.

"Really? That's funny, I remember you being interested in Darla, Jen, Tammy, Lisa—"

"Alright!" I cut her off there. "I get your point. But I wasn't really 'interested' in them. We just hung out. I was always honest that I wasn't looking for a relationship."

"And you are now?" Laney challenges me with sharp blue eyes.

"Maybe I met someone I actually want to be with." I hint.

"Oh, really? I would love to meet her."

"I think you know her pretty well. She goes to school with us. She has dark hair with red streaks and big, beautiful, blue eyes. I call her Lemon." There. I said it. A weight has been lifted, for now.

"And she hates it, sort of." Laney stares at me with mixed emotions.

"Why do you hate it?"

"Because, I don't know if it's just to toy with me or if you're actually serious about your feelings."

"I liked you from the moment I met you."

"You like a lot of girls, Kam."

"Not the way I like you." I sit up and put my plate down as I take Laney's out of her hand. I'm going to be bold. I grab Laney's wrist and pull her to me. She gasps but doesn't pull away as I trap her against my body.

"Kam—" She's tense in my arms. Her heart is beating against my chest and the smell of her flowery perfume is enlivening all my senses.

"Shhh." I drop my head down so my mouth is an inch away from hers. This is my megaphone, screaming loud and clear that I want her. That I need her. "Laney, all I'm asking is that you give me a chance. One chance."

"One chance at what?" She whispers back.

"To show you I'm not the guy you think I am."

She looks up at me with those big, blue eyes and I melt. I'm hers, there's no question. Now all I need is for her to be mine.

"Fine, Kam." She eyes me speculatively, a hint of humor dancing on her lips. "I'll give you a chance to prove it."

"You will?" I sound a little more surprised than I mean to.

"Yes." She giggles.

I lean in to kiss her, but she stops me by placing a finger on my mouth. "No. Prove to me we can hang out because you want *me* and not just my body."

"I want all of you," I divulge truthfully.

"Okay, then. So, tonight it's just pizza and Xbox and if you're a good boy, I'll give you a kiss."

"With tongue?"

"With tongue. I might even rub up against you."

"I can't wait to start being good."

Laney brushes her lips across mine. My body goes berserk. "A good faith gesture."

I'm left utterly speechless. I've never encountered anyone so audacious, yet reserved, coy, and fearlessly transparent. Laney has me in awe.

"Ready to get your butt kicked in Halo, country boy?"

"Absolutely. Just as long as you'll massage it after the beating."

"I can't make any promises."

"I can." I grab her face and plant a firm kiss right on her mouth. A little moan vibrates through her, and I'm elated. She melts against my body as I deepen the kiss just enough to tell her I want this. Want her.

"I really hope you're not fucking around, Kam," Laney breathes with her eyes still closed after I pull away.

"I'm not." She flutters her eyelashes and shows me those penetrable sky blues. They're the most susceptible I've ever seen them. Soft and hopeful. It's the first time she's allowing me see the emotion hidden behind her untrusting exterior. "Shall we let the ass-kicking commence?"

She bites her lip as if contemplating something.

"What?" I ask, trying to figure out what's going on in that head of hers.

"What if I kicked your ass later and kissed you now?"

"I'd say whatever you want, I want."

"Good answer, all-star." Laney crawls on top of me and straddles my legs. My hormones go haywire as she presses her lips to mine, urgently sucking and tasting. I wrap my arms around her waist and flex my hips, letting her know exactly what she's doing to me. She moans as our tongues clash together, rolling and flicking, forcing our bodies to grind together in a fit of passion.

I much prefer the kissing to the ass kicking.

I had no idea Friday night was going to be so much fun.

I HOLD THE FOOTBALL, palming it in one hand. It feels different. A stranger rather than the friend I had come to know. Some kids sleep with security blankets or stuffed animals when they're young. I slept with a football tucked in my arm, dreaming about touchdown passes and the roar of the crowd. I always knew this was my destiny. What I was meant to do.

I fire the ball at the tire swing, aiming for the hole and barely hit the perimeter. "*Goddamn it!*" I used to be able to throw pass after pass and hit my target every time. Now, I need to say a Hail Mary just to get it in the general vicinity. This is so fucking frustrating, and I can't figure out what's wrong. I have no control, and no matter how hard I concentrate, my 'pinpoint accuracy' is just gone, which makes my future and my life *gone*.

"Kam!" Laney calls from behind me. I turn to see my silver-lining walking toward me. Her dark hair is down and flipping in the wind, a wide smile brightening her face. In such a short time, I've come to live for that expression. It's rare, but when it happens, it's like looking at pure gold.

Seven days. That's how long Laney and I have been together. And despite my obvious adversity, when I'm with her, the world doesn't feel so dismal. "I was ringing the doorbell for like ten minutes."

"Sorry, I forgot my mom has book club tonight." I peck her on the lips. "How did you know I was back here?"

"I heard you curse. I didn't think good 'ol boys took God's name in vain, only sinful, city folk."

"You've been living in Alabama too long, Lemon. You're starting to talk like us." I wrap my arms around her waist and pull her into me, inhaling the strawberry scent of her hair.

"It was bound to rub off on me eventually."

"I have something I can rub on you."

"I might like that." She kisses my neck.

"Don't tease me, woman. We have the house to ourselves tonight."

"Who's teasing?" She looks up at me deviously.

"Hellcat." I grab her ass so hard I nearly pull her off the ground, and she squeaks. "How was practice?" Yup, Laney made the volleyball team and I can't wait to cheer her on.

"Fine. How was your day?"

"Uneventful." I glance down at the snake pit of footballs in the bin beside us.

"Still can't throw right?" she asks sympathetically.

"That's one way to put it," I respond sourly.

"Show me." She urges.

"Show you what?" I regard her confused.

"Show me how to throw a football."

"Are you being serious?" I raise my eyebrows.

"Yes. Don't think I can do it?" She puts her hands on her hips.

"I didn't say that. I just never expected those words to come out of your mouth. I'm totally turned on." I blink rapidly.

"Foreplay." Laney playfully reaches into the bin and pulls out a football. "Now, show me." She turns the ball in her tiny hands, and I don't think I've ever seen anything sexier in my life. I've never dated anyone who played sports before, unless you count cheerleading. The fact that

Laney is even entertaining the idea has my stomach doing back flips. I turn her around so her back is flush against my front.

"Okay, pay attention, this is rocket science," I warn. She giggles and presses her body harder against mine. It takes all the effort I can muster to concentrate on what I'm trying to do. Laney is very distracting. Especially when she's this close and smells this good and is finally all mine.

"First, your grip. Spread your fingers over the ball, two fingers between the laces." I place my hand over hers. "Make sure there's some air between your palm and the leather."

"Like this?" She listens impeccably and has a good hold on the ball.

"Just like that." I smile. This is way too much fun.

"Next, stand with your feet apart and your knees slightly bent." I turn her body sideways, never removing my arms from around her. "Now bring your arm up ninety degrees and pull the ball back. Keep everything tight. When you throw, bring your left elbow forward for momentum and push the ball off your index finger and thumb, rotating it under so it spirals." I walk her through the motions with my hands and body so she can correlate my words to the movements.

"Geez, you weren't kidding when you said it was rocket science," Laney jokes.

"Once you get the hang of it, it's as easy as breathing."

"So says the all-star quarterback."

"The former all-star quarterback," I correct her.

"I don't see a former anybody," Laney states simply, practicing what I just showed her. She has decent form, I'll give her that.

"Ready to fire this pigskin?" I grin.

"Let's do it." She pumps herself up.

"Once, together." I circle my arms back around her, place my right hand over hers on the ball and position my left arm, taking her hand in mine. Two bodies one motion, sort of like having sex. Laney wasn't kidding when she said foreplay. I'm totally turned on. I pull her arm back, and in one fluid motion we throw the ball. The spiral is a little off, but it hits the tire close to the hole. I think that was my best throw of the day.

"Okay, got it. Let me try." Laney pulls another ball out of the blue bin. I watch entertained as she positions her hands and takes her stance. Holy crap, I can't control the bulge growing behind my zipper. I'm fucking loving this.

Laney concentrates on the tire hanging a few meters away from us. I think I'm finally getting a glimpse of Sporty Spice. I can't wait to see her on the volleyball court. She snaps her arm back, and with all her might, throws the football. It teeters in the air, not quite getting a good spin, but hits the tire, nonetheless. No, not a terrible first shot.

"Crap." Laney goes for another ball.

"What, that wasn't bad."

"That sucked." Her voice pitches.

"It hit the tire," I point out.

"It didn't spin. And I didn't get it through the hole."

"Lemon, that's expecting a lot your first try."

She shoots me a death glare. Holy hell, my girl is a competitor. I guess I should have known that. She's been going head-to-head with me since the moment I met her.

Laney winds up again, her eyes keen as she focuses on the tire. She throws the ball and this time it spins beautifully through the air. It bounces off the tire and dies on the ground.

"Nice, Lemon." I clap. "That's how to do it."

"Once more." She goes for another football. My face lights up. I could watch this all night. Laney grips the football with both hands like she's trying to become familiar with the feel of the leather. I can't wait till she touches me like that. If I have anything to say about it, it will be tonight. My whole body is throbbing from just the thought. Once she's done, she takes her stance, angling her body and drawing the football up behind her head. The fire in her eyes is bright. Laney hurls the ball and it once again rotates perfectly though the air, except this time, instead of bouncing off the rubber of the tire, it soars straight through the hole.

"Yes!" Laney jumps into my arms.

"Fuck me." My mouth is hanging open. She did it. The first time ever throwing a football and she sinks it. "Did you just play me, city girl?"

"No. I just had a good teacher." She wraps her legs around my waist. I'm not buying it.

"You lying?" I probe.

"Nope. I hate liars. You really are a good teacher. And I'm a little athletic, so I'm sure that helped." She beams.

"I think it did." I kiss her neck. She moans and the strain in my pants can't take it anymore. I turn toward the house and start walking.

"Kam! Put me down! You're going to hurt yourself!"

"Don't be ridiculous, I'm fine." I march through the back door with Laney still latched on to me. "I go back to school on Monday. I'm cleared for physical activity."

"And what kind of physical activity did you have in mind?" she asks as I walk up the steps toward my room.

"The kind that involves a bed."

"Kam, I'm not going to sleep with you."

"Who said anything about sleeping, sugar?"

"Don't call me sugar." She is seriously testy about that nickname.

"Sorry. Lemon," I correct myself.

"Better." She kisses me. I've waited to be alone with Laney ever since last Friday night. And now that I have her all to myself, I'm going to take full advantage. I flip her onto the mattress causing her to giggle-scream as she falls backwards. I yank my shirt off right before I crawl onto the bed. Laney's eyes widen, and her lips part.

"Something wrong, Lemon?" I pause.

"Nope, not a thing. Just admiring."

"Like what you see?" I slowly creep over her body.

"Mmmm-hmmm." I lie on top of her and crush my mouth against hers. She opens immediately, allowing my tongue to explore. Rolling and circling it slowly, I take possession of the woman beneath me. The girl I've wanted from the first second I saw her.

"You know it's not fair you're still wearing a shirt," I hint between kisses.

"So, take it off."

I don't waste a second ripping Laney's shirt off, or her bra for that matter. Her skin is fucking beautiful, and so, so soft. I trail my tongue down her neck as I massage one of her breasts in my hand. I suck her nipple into my mouth and swirl my tongue, causing it to pebble. "Kam," she moans as I lavish each breast, her hands gripping the strands of my hair. If she thinks that feels good, just wait. I move farther down until I reach the button of her jeans. I pop it open and Laney pushes herself up on her elbows. "Kam."

"Don't worry, I heard you when you said you weren't going to sleep with me. Doesn't mean I can't make you feel good other ways." I grin devilishly. I don't even wait for a response as I suck on her flesh. Laney lies back down as I remove her pants, then her cotton underwear with little stars without delay. I wanted Laney naked, and that's exactly how I'll have her. "Fuck, you're so hot." I drop down, placing light kisses below her belly button at the same time rubbing her clit with the pad of my thumb. Her body bows and a little moan escapes her mouth. Laney spreads her legs, and I take it as an invitation. In my world, there's more than one way to fuck. I replace my finger with my tongue without any warning and slash at Laney's flesh. She suddenly gasps, "Oh, God." Working my mouth as Laney squirms I build her up to exactly where I want her. Wet and wanton and trembling under my command.

After a few heat-induced minutes, I go in for the kill and slide one finger inside her. She bucks her hips and grabs at the headboard as I lick and finger her into an orgasm. Her muscles clench so sweetly as she screams my name while she detonates on the bed. Her body seizing as her climax takes hold. Once I'm satisfied I have wrung out every drop of her arousal, I kiss my way back up her body. She locks her arms around my neck and hooks one leg around mine, sighing contentedly. She's not the only happy one. I've never enjoyed giving pleasure as much as the person receiving it. Everything with Laney is different. I spend the next few minutes exploring Laney's sated body, running my fingers along the curve of her hips and the swell of her breasts. Her exotic scent filling my senses. She feels so good, so right.

"My turn, all-star." Laney sucks on my neck, sending a shiver down my spine.

"Your turn for what?" I murmur.

"To play." She slips her hands between us and unbuttons my fly. She's not going to get any arguments from me. I roll off Laney and allow her to remove my pants, underwear and all. "That's better. Level playing field." She gropes me with her eyes. I eat up the fact she loves my body. She then shifts off the bed and kneels on the floor. Laney naked and on her knees nearly makes me combust. I slide forward, planting both feet on the ground, Laney smack dab between my legs. I slide my fingers into her hair and kiss her reverently. I don't think she has any idea how much she means to me. But I'm going to do my best every day to tell her.

Laney runs her hands along my chest and over my abs. Her fingers outlining my six pack. Her touch is electric; it has every one of my nerve-endings humming. When she grazes my erection, it forces a moan from my throat. I'm over-stimulated and sensitive as hell. Laney breaks our kiss as she holds my cock tightly, all the blood rushing to the tip of my head. I'm nothing but sensation as she takes me in her mouth. She swirls her tongue and sucks hard, causing me to see stars. I grip her hair as she swallows me over and over until I'm dangling right over the edge. "Laney," I grit out trying to warn her my climax is coming, and soon. She only sucks harder and faster causing all my muscles to stiffen. "Fuck, baby." I choke.

Seconds later I explode, the whole world falling away, as I come violently in her mouth. I fall back on the bed completely drained as Laney licks up every drop of my orgasm.

"Come here." I hold my arms out, half conscious. I just need to hold her. Laney climbs up over my naked body and snuggles up against me. "Mmmm." I love having nothing between us. Laney and I just lounge, stroking and caressing each other in comfortable silence. A guy could totally get used to this.

"We better get dressed," Laney disrupts the silence way too soon.

I know she's right, my mom will be home soon, but I'm just not ready to let her go. "One more minute."

She humors me.

"Laney?"

"Yeah, Kam?"

"If I never played football again, would that be okay with you?" I don't know what spurs the question. Old demons, maybe.

Laney stops tracing my stomach and lifts her head to look at me. Her hair is a bit messy and there is a red-streaked strand falling over her right eye. "Of course it would. I don't care that you play football, Kam. I only care that you're happy." I nod. I only care that she's happy, too. "And I have complete faith you'll play football again. The question is, do you want to?"

"More than anything." I don't even hesitate.

"Then you will."

"I hope so." I stare at the ceiling. I don't know how one aspect of my life can be so perfect and the other be such a mess.

Laney lies back down and hugs me tight. Her touch alone is medicinal. "My father was watching this football movie the other night. I don't know the name of it," she starts. "I was only half paying attention. But I remember the coach being interviewed by a reporter. She asked what his team was missing. I guess they weren't very good or something."

"What was his reply?" I ask, intrigued.

"Heart. He said they were missing heart." She looks up at me. "Do you have heart, Kam?"

I stare at Laney. Do I? I thought I did. But ever since the aneurysm, heart seems to be missing.

"I used to."

"Where is it now?"

I smile at her stupidly. "In my arms."

Chapter SIX

I WALK DOWN THE empty hallway.

It's my first day back at school, and I couldn't be more thrilled. One, because it gets me out of the house—I was starting to suffer from cabin fever. Two, because I get to spend first period with Laney, then lunch, then I get to enjoy watching her bounce around in little shorts during volleyball practice. Sometimes it doesn't totally suck to be Kamdyn Ellis.

I stroll past the lockers toward chem when someone grabs me by the arm. "Whoa!" I'm yanked into the storage room and attacked by a pair of sugary, sweet tasting lips. They smash against mine, and I'm momentarily stunned. "*Darla?* What the fuck?" I push her away. Seriously, did this chick not get the message? I haven't called or texted or even breathed in her direction in months, and yet here she is shoving her tongue down my throat.

"I've been waiting for you. I wanted to be the first to welcome you back," she purrs.

"A simple hi would have been fine." I wipe her sticky lip gloss off my mouth. *Yuck.* Darla pouts. I've been back at school for five seconds, and it's starting already.

"What's wrong with you, Kam? You're no fun anymore."

"I'm plenty fun, sugar. I'm just not interested in having any with you. I tried to be nice, but that didn't seem to work. So, let me be clear. I don't like you. I don't want to fool around or hang out. I have a girlfriend now. And I don't think she'd take too kindly to you accosting me in the storage closet."

"A girlfriend?" Darla squeaks, and then it registers. "Laney Summers?" She almost sounds disgusted.

"Yes, Laney Summers. You have a problem with that?"

"No." Darla backs down. "She just doesn't seem like your type."

"Yeah, well opposites attract. Now, back off."

The warning bell rings.

"Fine. I'm sorry." She retreats backwards, hugging herself.

"If you want to apologize to someone, do it to Laney." I bite.

"You going to tell her?"

"Afraid she'll kick your ass?"

"No," Darla huffs.

"You should be. She's tough. Trust me, I know. I've wrestled with her." Darla scrunches her nose. Didn't like that mental picture, huh? I grin to myself.

"So, are you going to tell her?" Darla sounds a little more alarmed now. And she should be. I wasn't kidding when I said Laney was tough. She can definitely throw down.

"Are you going to leave me alone?" I press.

"Yes."

"Then, no. Let's keep both our asses out of trouble."

"Fine." She agrees.

"Good." I open the door to a hallway full of my peers. I don't make it two steps into the crowd when I run right into the person I most wanted to see . . . just not at this moment.

Laney's eyes widen as she looks between me and Darla. This is not good. So not good. So, so not good.

"No, Laney. It's not what you think." I panic.

"Oh, really? Because it looks like you and Darla coming out of the storage room after a morning hook-up." She gets shoved by someone and loses her footing. I grab her before she falls. "No. Laney."

"Don't touch me!" she snaps, pulling away. "God, you really are a douchebag." She calls me out in the middle of the hallway, stopping pedestrian traffic. Fuck. Just what we need—an audience.

"Can we talk about this someplace else?" I lower my voice so only she can hear me.

"Talk? You think I want to talk to you? Shit, Kam, you really had me fooled." She sounds so hurt. But it's not what she thinks. If I can just explain!

"I never lied to you!"

"Are you seriously trying to play that card?" she hisses, disgusted.

The bell rings again, and everyone starts to scatter. Half the school is late for first period. Laney takes off, and I rush after her. "Laney! Laney!"

She walks into chem and straight to Mr. Johnson's desk. "Can I have a pass for the nurse, please?" Her voice cracks. *Shit. No!*

"Is everything alright, Ms. Summers?" the older man with white hair asks as he writes it out.

"Fine. I'm just suddenly not feeling so well." She snatches the small, pink piece of paper out of his hand,

"Do you need someone to take you?"

"I will," I interject.

"No!" Laney seethes. Mr. Johnson looks between us concerned. "I'm fine, really. I just need to go now."

"I'll mark you as present. Go ahead." Laney walks out the door, and I follow.

"Laney," I voice, desperate for her to just look at me. She has it all wrong.

"Piss off, Kam," she growls.

She's gone after that.

"Fuck!" I punch a locker.

What was I saying about it not sucking to be Kamdyn Ellis? *FUMBLE!*

I'VE TRIED EVERYTHING.

Cards, flowers, candy. Nothing works. Laney has officially cut me off. It's been over a month, and she's barely spoken three words to me.

Chem is worse than Chinese water torture. Sitting half a foot away from the person you love, and them not giving you the time of day is cruel and unusual punishment.

Life has just been fucking fabulous lately. I lost my girl *and* the ability to play football. Why doesn't the universe just take my hands, feet, eyes, and ears, and call it a day. This mundane, slow death is agonizing.

Laney comes into first period and sits next to me in her usual seat. She drops her book bag on the table, pulls out her notebook, and looks straight ahead. Not even a glance in my direction.

"Hey," I say.

"Hey," she responds coolly, just to be polite. That is what our relationship has become—a series of distant pleasantries. I watch her out of the corner of my eye as Mr. Johnson lectures about chemical reaction and mass conservation. I'm not hearing a word. The only chemical reaction I'm interested in is the one that happens when Laney is in my arms. She jots down her notes diligently, her dark hair hiding most of her face. I want to reach out and tuck it behind her ear just so I can see her.

"Lemon," I whisper, but she ignores me. "Lemon, can we please talk?"

"There's nothing to talk about," she responds harshly.

"I think there is." She keeps her eyes forward, unrelenting. It makes me crazy. "Laney, I miss you."

That gets her attention. She stares at me with those bold blue eyes. I wonder if that put a chink in her armor. But she only scowls. "Then you should have thought about that before you went into the storage room with Darla."

"I didn't choose to go in, she grabbed me. And nothing happened, just like I told you a hundred times."

"I wish I could believe you, Kam." She drops her head mournfully, scribbling in her notebook.

"Why can't you?" I dispute.

"Because leopards don't change their spots. And I can't be with someone who cheats on me. Call me possessive, I like what's mine."

"I am yours. And I would never cheat on you. That's not who I am."

"I don't know who you are."

Ouch.

I shake my head furiously. "You are the only person who knows me."

Laney frowns. "Just leave it alone, Kam. It's over."

It's hard to accept. Defeat never comes easily to a competitor.

Chapter SEVEN

GRADUATION IS TWO WEEKS away.

The school is buzzing with excitement as the valedictorian is announced, the gym is prepared for the ceremony, and college acceptance letters pour in. I knew which college I was going to my junior year, the day the head coach of the University of Alabama came to my house with an offer I couldn't refuse. That day changed everything. If I was star before, I was a god now. I wasn't kidding when I told Laney football is a religion around here. Bear Bryant is Alabama's messiah, and the fans are his followers. Roll Tide was the foundation of my football dream. There's countless t-shirts packed in my drawers. A collection of ambitions: 'Built by Bama', 'Keep Calm, The Tide is Coming', 'Heart and Soul Crimson Tide is How I Roll'. But soon, they'll mean nothing; a vigil to the future that died that day on the football field.

I can't throw, my accuracy is gone—a neurological side effect of the aneurysm. I'll have to face the truth when I look into the eyes of the man who offered me everything and tell him my career is over before it even began.

I'm just not ready to do that though. So I'm going to try to distract myself for the next two weeks with senior year festivities, starting with the annual Powder Puff football game this afternoon.

I'm a male cheerleader—the best looking one in the bunch, too. I'll be on the sidelines chanting as a group of handpicked girls go head-to-head with our rival school, North. You know them. I kicked their ass in the state championship.

The other 'cheerleaders' and I wait on one side of the huge banner by the south end zone. Just like when we play, the girls will burst through the crepe paper and run onto the field. Our team is called the Alabama Slammers. I thought it was catchy.

This is the first time I've stepped foot in this stadium since the state final. It all feels the same—overwhelming, awe-inspiring, adrenaline pumping. I miss it every single day.

The band starts to play our fight song, signaling the start of the game. The players barrel through the decorated paper that declares GO ALABAMA BLUE. Each girl is dressed in a navy midriff jersey and black shorts. Their hair is done up in ponytails or pigtails with W for Wolverines painted on their faces. I take my place on the sidelines, luckily dressed in jeans and a pink t-shirt, instead of a cheerleading skirt like the bozos on the other team. I take an inventory of the starting lineup. That's when it hits me like a battering ram to the chest. Laney, standing next to Coach McKenzie, is taking direction on plays. Her dark hair is in two, low pigtails and there's a swipe of eye black under each of her eyes. But it's the number on her chest that has me panting. A huge, white seven is blaring back at me. Is she the QB? I didn't even know she was playing. I make my way over to her and the head coach of the Wolverine's, the man who has led seven teams to the state championships in ten years. To say he is respected would be an understatement. We don't mess around in these parts. If we're going to play football, whether it be Powder Puff or not, we call in the big guns. I eavesdrop as he goes over the running and passing plays. She looks a little nervous, but also intense. Her competitive side is flaring. It's the same when she plays volleyball. You can see the hunger to win in her eyes. How do I know? I may have stalked a game or two. Sue me, I missed her.

After the coin toss, and right before the players take the field, I pull Laney aside. "When did you decide to play?"

"I didn't."

"I don't understand."

"I tossed a football around with Miranda before one of her practices. Coach McKenzie saw me and I didn't have a choice after that," she explains, irked. Miranda is the tiny bubbly blonde wearing the number nineteen. She's a wide receiver. I know she'll probably kick ass catching passes. Her boyfriend, Logan, is an all-state tight end. I'm sure he gave her a few pointers. I would have done the same for Laney if I knew she was QB.

"Our little lesson paid off." I can't help but smile proudly.

"Apparently so." She sounds like she regrets ever picking up a football. It hurts my heart.

"You're wearing my number. How did that happen?" She glares at me. The sun making her blue irises crystallize.

Laney shrugs. "It's a quarterback's number."

"There are lots of quarterback numbers, why that one?"

She's reluctant to answer as Coach McKenzie barks at her to get on the field. "It has heart."

I watch her hustle away and take her place in the huddle. I feel like I'm soaring, dangerously close to believing a chance at reconciliation isn't dead after all.

We won the coin toss, so the Slammers have the ball. I watch mesmerized as the girls line up. They look so little on that huge field. Laney stands behind the center whom I recognize from the lacrosse team. She's got some girth. Laney calls hike, and the ball is snapped into her hands. She shuffles, looking for an open receiver when she's sacked. Hard. Shit.

She didn't even see it coming. It takes her a second to get up. I want to run out onto the field and make sure she's okay. But she makes it to her feet and goes right back in. *Fight, Laney, you have to fight.*

The next play Laney is able to pass, but it's incomplete, just inches away from Miranda's fingers. This goes on for two more downs. It's the third down and the ball hasn't advanced at all. I hear coach call a running play. A 134 Sweep on the outside. Laney will have to run it. I hear her repeat in the huddle, her little voice already hoarse from yelling. The line takes position and Laney screams hike. The girls block left and right, making a tiny opening for Laney to sneak through. I hold my breath as she gets lost in shoving bodies then reemerges with the football tucked in her arm. She books it down the field, with two linemen—excuse me, line women—hot on her tail. I find myself screaming, along with everyone else, as Laney is tackled right on the five-yard line. Nice breakaway!

We're in scoring position.

Coach calls another play. We all feel the excitement. Scoring is a rush.

Laney crouches behind the center and calls hike. Miranda makes it into the end zone, and Laney fires it. *Touchdown!*

Then she's tackled. For no good reason. "What the fuck! Unnecessary roughness!"

"Ellis! Mouth," Coach McKenzie reprimands me.

"She was just sacked after the TD! Where's the penalty?"

"It's going to be up your ass if you don't zip it and cheer." He looks back at me and scowls.

I flip him the finger. Inside my head.

Laney takes a seat on the bench, and I bring her some water. "Is it this nerve-wracking watching me play?"

"Yes," she takes a big gulp. "Especially when you don't get up after you're tackled."

I frown. "I didn't mean to worry anyone."

"We're not worried anymore. And it's all part of the game, right?"

She huffs, out of breath.

"I'm learning it's all part of life. Take a hit, get right back up."

"I'll remember that next time number sixty-seven steamrolls me." Laney rolls her shoulder and stretches her neck.

"They're a little aggressive, huh?"

"They're out for blood. One of the girls said she overheard the defense talking about retribution for state. And they're all gunning for me."

"Shit," I spit.

"Summers!" Coach calls. Offense has the ball.

"Any last minute pointers before I go back out there?" she asks.

"Yeah, avoid getting tackled at all costs."

"Oh, that's a big help." She chucks the paper cup at me and runs onto the field. I won't lie, I like looking at her ass in those tight shorts. We finally have a common interest in the sport.

For the next two quarters I proceed to watch Laney get her ass handed to her. Literally. North is playing dirty as hell. I've made sure to voice my opinion on the matter, repeatedly.

By the fourth quarter, Laney looks wiped. Her pigtails are a mess, she's covered in grass stains, and I think she hurt her left elbow. She won't admit it though, no matter how much I badger her about it. She's a warrior, I'll give her that. Watching this game has solidified my feelings for her. There's no doubt in my mind she's the girl I have to be with.

There's two minutes left on the clock, and we're down by six. This game has been full-on war. North's team is on steroids or something; they hit harder than the guys.

It's third down on the five-yard line, and we have an opportunity to score. Laney tries for a pass, but it's incomplete.

"Run! She has to run it!" I boisterously tell Coach McKenzie. I've secured a position on the sideline right next to him. So much for cheerleading. I wasn't that into it anyway. Too much testosterone.

"Can it, Ellis," Coach smirks. "I'm going to run it."

He calls out the play. It's short and sweet. Nothing like the paragraphs

I needed to memorize on a weekly basis: 35 liberty west right flanker out pop eighty hot yellow yellow void java java right flat.

Laney gets 138 Blast, straight up the middle.

The line sets up, and Laney yells hike. She barrels through the wall of bodies only to get shut down on the two-yard line. *Fuck!* This is anxiety at its best. I know she can do this! Coach tries to call another running play, but I interrupt him. "A draw. Run a draw!" They both look at me like I'm nuts.

"She's on the two-yard line with ninety seconds left on the clock," he argues with me. We have no timeouts left, so I have to make my argument quick.

"Exactly. They'll never expect it. What do we have to lose?"

"The game, genius!"

"Lemon, run the play!" I yell to her from the sideline and Coach throws up his hands. She nods.

"I suppose you want to take over coaching next year, too?" he asks exasperated.

"Nah, I'll be in college by then. Gotta have a little fun before I die." I wink at him.

"With or without college, Ellis, I don't think you'll have any shortage on fun."

I shush him playfully. "Gotta watch my girl score a touchdown."

"I didn't realize you were dating." Coach arches an eyebrow.

"She doesn't realize it either, but I'm changing that tonight." I vow.

Coach scoffs. "Good luck with that. It looked like she wanted to scratch your eyes out before."

"She did." I smile. "City girl—thinks she's tough."

"From what I saw today, she is." He stands stoically on the sideline, arms crossed.

That makes me smile even more.

Laney yells hike, and I watch, with all the air subdued in my lungs, as she drops back like she's going to pass, then fakes and hands the ball to the running back behind her. The tall blonde finds a hole in the line and runs seamlessly into the end zone.

TOUCHDOWN!

Everyone on the sidelines and in the stands goes berserk.

"Alright, alright! No celebration yet, we're still down by one!" Coach McKenzie screams. He sends in the kicker. This is in the bag. I've seen Sherry punt, she's a soccer player who can launch the ball seventy-five yards.

The line quickly reforms. My heart is beating out of my chest. North looks burned up. They came for retribution, and all they got was another ass kicking. When will they learn?

The center snaps the ball, and Laney positions it laces out. Sherry kicks and all eyes follow as it soars perfectly between the goal posts.

Wolverines twenty-eight; North twenty-seven. *Losers.*

The Slammers run off the field animated and victorious. Laney jumps into my arms as soon as she reaches me. I'm not sure what sparked it, but I'm not going to look a gift horse in the mouth.

"You kicked butt, QB."

"I had a stellar offensive coach." Laney tries to slide down my body, but I stop her. I'm not letting her go. Ever again.

"Kam, put me down."

"No."

"Come on." She kicks her legs, but I still refuse her.

"We need to talk."

"There's nothing to talk about. Besides, I need ice for my elbow."

"You did hurt it." I stare her down. I would have iced it a quarter and a half ago. "Fine, we'll get ice, and we'll talk." I march straight off the field, down the throughway and into the locker room.

"Kam! This is the boys' locker room, I can't be in here!"

"Of course, you can. No one's here. Besides, this stadium has the best rehab room in the state." I plant Laney on the bench in front of my old locker. She looks around as I retrieve an ice pack, a thin towel, and some wrap. "Put your arm out," I instruct. She does, and I carefully place the wrapped ice pack against her elbow and wind the bandage around it. "Better?"

She looks at her arm. "It's good. Thanks."

"Welcome. Now, let's talk." I straddle the bench so we are sitting face to face.

"About what?"

"Us."

Laney huffs. "There is no us."

"Well, there should be." I debate.

"I can't be with someone I can't trust."

"Damn it, Laney, you can trust me." I slam the locker beside me with my fist. She jumps. "Have you seen me with one other girl since we broke up? And don't say Darla, because that doesn't count. Nothing happened."

"No," she answers.

"And why do you think that is?"

"No fresh meat?" She digs.

I groan. "Are all city girls as frustrating as you?"

"Yes, it's part of our charm."

That causes me to crack a smile. "Do you want to know why I messed around with all those girls?"

"Do I want to know?" She curls her lip.

"Yes. Maybe it will give you some perspective. You know who my ex is, right?"

"Of course, everyone knows who Cheyenne is. Head cheerleader, prom queen, student body president."

"Yup, that's her. She's also self-centered, egotistical, and a mega bitch. I spent three years of my life with a girl who didn't give two shits about me. All she cared about was her social status and what I could do for it. I finally had enough when she showed up to my grandfather's funeral two hours late and didn't even kiss me hello or offer her condolences to my father. Who wants to date a person like that? So, I dumped her, vowing I was going to spend my senior year having fun and not be tied down."

"Well, it sort of worked out that way," Laney comments.

"Yeah, everything was going fine until a smart-mouthed, city girl with blue eyes and crazy streaked hair strolled into first period and sat next to me. I was attracted to you the first second I saw you, and you wouldn't give me the time of day."

"You shouldn't have called me sugar right off the bat." She shrugs.

"I call everyone sugar. It's habit."

"Exactly. I didn't want to be part of your bad habit. I didn't want to be another girl on your roster."

"You had to know you weren't just another girl."

"For a second, I thought I was different."

"You are." I grab her hand. It feels so good in mine. "And I'm collecting on our bet. I'm not letting you get away again."

"Bet?" She raises her eyebrows.

"Yeah, the one we made in chem the morning of the state championships. If I recall, we won *and* covered the spread."

"You're devious." She leers.

"Yup, and I want you."

"That bet was just my body. No strings attached." She reminds me.

"We can start there, Lemon. You got a taste of what I can do to your body." Laney's eyes flash. "And that was just the tip of the iceberg." I lean in and brush my lips against hers. She stiffens, fighting me. "What do you say? Will you give me one night to prove myself?"

Laney looks up at me with confliction in her eyes. "One night, Kam," she sighs, giving in.

"That's all I need."

Chapter EIGHT

LANEY CLIMBS INTO MY pickup a little after ten pm.

She wouldn't let me come to the door, even though I insisted.

"I can't believe your father let you walk out of the house without meeting me. It feels rude. I didn't even get to shake his hand."

"One, my father's in New York. And two, he only shakes the hands of guys I believe are going to stick around." She slams the passenger's side door.

"You have the wrong impression of me, Lemon."

"Well, isn't that what tonight's for? To prove that impression wrong?"

"Yup." I throw the truck into D and pull away.

"Where are we going, anyway?"

"For a little drive." I grin slyly.

"You know when you say that to a New Yorker they become extremely paranoid."

I look at her funny.

"That's a mafia joke." She explains.

"Oh. I don't think we have any Sopranos in these parts."

She snickers.

I drive around for about a half hour before we pull up to our destination.

"The football stadium?" Laney looks at me, confused.

"Yup." I park off to the side, in the dark, so my pickup isn't noticed. I'd like to avoid any interruptions. Laney and I get out of the truck, and I grab the two blankets and cooler from the cab. She follows as I walk down a dark path.

"Are you sure I don't have anything to be worried about?" Laney sounds slightly paranoid.

"Not when you're with me, Lemon." I slip through an opening in the fence. It's by the dumpsters so there's not the most appealing smell in the air, but we will be far away from it soon enough. "Every year there's a field party thrown by the seniors. This is how we sneak in."

A few minutes later we're walking onto the end zone. Laney does a little turn, looking up. "God, you never see this many stars in the city."

"Beauty of country living." It's dark on the field, but the sky is twinkling with a billion platinum dots and a huge, full moon that's casting a silvery light. There's just enough illumination to see and still enough darkness to hide us.

"And it's crazy the Wolverines have their own stadium. Most schools just have a field."

"We're not most schools. We've won state nineteen times."

"Quite a legacy to leave behind," she muses. I frown. She has no idea, especially if I'm never going to play football again. I walk Laney across the field over the ten, twenty, and thirty-yard lines until we finally reach the fifty. The dead center of the universe. Well, my universe. I lay out one of the blankets and drop the cooler. It's colder than one would expect an Alabama night to be, but the smell of the fresh-cut grass is as potent as ever. I inhale deeply—it's almost as heady as Laney's exotic scent.

I motion for Laney to sit. Once situated, I open the cooler and pull out two cups and an orange Gatorade water bottle. Laney shoots me a skeptical look.

"I promise it's not what you think." I pour her a cup, then one for myself.

"Okay, I trust you."

I pause. "Nice to know we're making progress." I clink my red Solo cup against hers. "To trust. And forgiveness."

"And playing football," Laney adds.

I die a little death. "You certainly played your heart out today."

"I didn't want to make the infamous number seven look bad."

"You could never make it look bad. You have no idea how long I've wanted to see you wear that number."

"Since the first moment you met me?" She bats her eyelashes.

"Something like that." I take a sip trying to hide my smile, and Laney does, too.

"Mmm, what is this?" she asks curiously, looking into the cup.

"You like it?"

"Yes." She takes another sip.

"Iced tea vodka and lemonade."

"Much better than sweet tea," she licks her lips.

"You don't like sweet tea?" I ask, a little shocked.

"You didn't notice I never drank anything at dinner when we were studying?"

"I did. I just never thought . . . I mean, I can't imagine anyone not liking sweet tea."

"I felt bad telling your mom I didn't like it."

"You really are a Yankee," I tease.

"Born and bred." She laughs.

"I forgive you," I joke.

"We can't all be perfect like you." She knocks her knees against mine.

"I'm not perfect anymore. Not that I ever was." I look up at the starry sky.

"You're too hard on yourself." I can feel Laney's eyes searing through me.

"I don't know any other way to be." I shrug. "My whole life I've been under a spotlight. People have either wanted something or expected something from me. I've always felt pressure to deliver."

"I see," she considers, taking another sip of her drink. I didn't mean to get deep, but it's easy to talk to Laney. Too easy sometimes.

"So, why is your dad in New York?" I clear my throat, my soul feeling a little too bare.

"He's guest starring on *America's Next Top Chef.* He's the celebrity judge."

"That sounds cool."

"Yeah, he asked me to go with him, but I couldn't bail on the football game. Miranda would have skinned me."

"You passed on a trip to New York to play Powder Puff football?" I raise my eyebrows.

"Why do you sound shocked?"

"Because I am." I laugh.

"Why?" she demands.

"Because football is just a game to you."

"True, but it's like a religion to the people around here. I didn't want them to burn me in effigy if I ducked out."

"They probably would have, too."

"I don't doubt it," she laughs. I love that sound. "I also couldn't pass up an opportunity to see you cheer on the sidelines."

"Oh, you couldn't?"

"Nope."

"What'd you think?"

"You disappointed me, all-star. You didn't give one hundred percent."

"Nope," I agree. "It wasn't really my thing."

"Annoying Coach McKenzie on the sidelines seemed to be your thing."

"I was assisting," I defend myself.

"I think it was more annoying." She contends.

"I helped win the game, didn't I?"

Laney rolls her eyes. "I guess."

"You guess?" I poke her in the ribs and she jumps, letting out a cute little squeak.

"That wasn't nice!" She pokes me back, harder than I expected.

"Oh, you asked for it." I toss my cup and pounce on her, tickling her sides. She squeals as some of her drink spills on her shirt and the grass.

"Kam!" she screams, kicking her legs around. "Uncle! Uncle!"

I let up on the tickling, but I don't get off her.

"You're so mean," she huffs, wiping off her t-shirt. *I love Laney wet.*

"Sometimes," I confirm. Then I lean in and kiss her. It's a test kiss, to see exactly where her head is. My assessment tells me a good place, because she opens her mouth and wraps her arms around my neck. Our tongues dance as I situate myself between her thighs. She sighs, deepening the kiss, causing it to become more urgent, fevered. I press against her, my want evident as she wraps her legs around my waist and draws me close. "God, I missed touching you." I slip my hand under her shirt, skimming my fingers up her side, until I reach the soft material of her bra. I cup her breast and squeeze lightly as she moans. Laney goes for the hem of my shirt, tugging it up so my stomach is exposed. She runs her hands up my sides and down my back, grazing her nails over my sensitive skin. Holy hell, her touch feels like trickles of water. Soft and enticing, inviting and alluring. My control completely liquefies.

"Laney," I rasp as I press my hips against her harder.

"Kam, shhh. You don't have to say anything. No strings, remember?"

I look down at her, our mouths a fraction of a centimeter apart. "What if I want the strings?"

"Then you can have them." She lifts her head and brushes her lips across mine. My whole being lights up. There's nothing at this moment I want more. Laney pulls my shirt over my head then goes for the button of my jeans. I love that she's not shy, that she knows exactly what she wants. Which, right now, is me.

After a few seconds of frenzied hands, we're both stripped completely naked. I grab the other blanket and cover us as I nestle myself back between her knees. Laney folds her arms around me, bringing us as close as we can possibly be. I touch every part of her I can, skin-to-skin, mouth-to-mouth. I slip my hand between our bodies and skim her clit with one finger. She whimpers. It spurs me on, so I slip the same finger inside her and her body tenses.

"Oh, God . . ." She digs her nails into my shoulders. I finger her slow and suck on her neck. "Kam, please not like this."

"Not like what? You have to tell me what you want, Laney."

"You. Only you." She attacks my mouth, and I almost combust. I reach for my pants and pull out my wallet, then two blue foil packets. Laney grabs one. She tears it open, removes the condom, then reaches down between us. I watch as she sheaths my erection, the feel of her hands is euphoric.

"Fuck, I need to be inside you." I pump my hips against her palm.

"No one is stopping you." She opens her legs a little wider. I love this girl. I am stupidly, ridiculously in love with Laney Summers. I push inside her gradually, savoring every measured inch. Her body welcoming me like a warm embrace. Laney wraps her legs around my waist, and we start to move, searching for a comfortable rhythm. After a minute or two we find it, and that's when all sense and reason fades away. There's only Laney; underneath me, folded around me, seeping inside me.

"Kam, you feel so good." She flexes her hips, like I can't thrust deep enough. Her muscles clench and her eyes close, as her breathing becomes choppy. "Please, don't stop."

"Never." I push her toward her orgasm, thrusting rhythmically, deeply, unyieldingly, giving her everything she demands from my body until she breaks. Being with Laney is beyond amazing; her smell, her sounds, the way she feels. It's sensation overload.

"Oh, God!" She finally comes in a rush, propelling my release. With my own climax threatening, I wring out every drop of ecstasy from her I can.

As she writhes and moans beneath me, my cock pulses until I explode, my body seizing in pure rapture. When my orgasm releases me, I drop down into Laney's waiting arms. She hugs me tight. I hug her back; inhaling her skin, skimming my teeth against her flesh, memorizing every luscious inch of her.

"Is that the first time you ever blew the whistle on the fifty-yard line?" she asks while gliding her fingers up and down my back.

I chuckle. "Yes. You?"

Laney laughs. "Definitely."

"How was it?"

"Unforgettable."

I peck her on the lips. I'm absurdly happy at the moment. And it's not because I just got laid.

I very reluctantly withdraw from Laney—I could stay buried in her all night—and roll onto my back, snuggling her into the crook of my arm. We lie quietly, me rubbing her hip, her rubbing my chest. For the first time in months, everything feels right. It's like when Laney is next to me my life is aligned. I kiss her head firmly, bindingly.

"What was that for?"

"Nothin.'" I shrug. "Can't a guy just kiss his girlfriend?"

She glances up at me. "Is that what I am?"

"Well, Lemon, when I said strings I wasn't talking about shoelaces."

"Glad you made that clear." She tightens her arm around me. I smile.

"Why do you always smell so good?" I breathe her in. That strange, exotic scent is tingling my senses.

"Because I shower."

I pinch her playfully. "Smart-ass city girl."

"Hey!" She flinches, giggling. "It's Plumeria."

"Plum-whatta?"

Now she is full-blown laughing. "It's a flower that grows in Hawaii. My mom always brings me back perfume when she goes."

"Hawaii, huh?" I stare into the black ocean above us glowing with stars. "She ever take you on her business trips?"

"If she can. And if I'm not in school. Why? Want to go to Hawaii?"

"Might not be a bad idea. I'm going to have some free time on my hands."

"Why is that?"

"Because I'm not going to play football anymore." That's the first time I've admitted that out loud. It feels like someone just stabbed me.

"Why aren't you going to play football anymore?" Laney asks softly, snuggling closer to me.

I huff. "Because I can't throw anymore, Lemon. My accuracy is gone. And without that, I'm no good to anyone."

Laney frowns. "Kam, you really believe your football career is over?"

I want to say no, but it's time to face facts. "I think it is."

Laney stares at me for a long minute. "How was it before you had the aneurysm?"

"How do you mean?"

"I mean, what did you do differently then compared to now?"

"Nothing. I just picked up a football and threw. I never had to think about it."

"Maybe that's your problem. You're so worried, you're overthinking it."

I gaze blankly at Laney. Overthinking it? Is that possible? "I never thought of it like that."

"Well, this night is all about new perspective, right?"

"I guess." I nuzzle her neck and nip at her skin.

My Lemon is smart, sassy, and now psychoanalytic. I hit the jackpot with this one.

Chapter NINE

I HOLD THE FOOTBALL in my hands as the dawn peeks out from the behind the horizon.

It's Monday morning. Laney and I spent the entire weekend together making up for lost time. I don't think seven days a week, twenty-four seven would be enough time to spend with Laney. The girl has me hooked, and there's no place I'd rather be. Except maybe on a football field. Preferably with Laney. Naked.

I roll the ball between my palms and inhale the smell of early morning. Everything is peaceful. Everything is quiet. I stare at the tire swing as pink light casts its luminescent glow.

Maybe you're overthinking it. Maybe she's right.

I close my eyes. What do I have to lose? Placing my fingers between the laces, I just let go; tossing the ball at the tire. I send every dream, every hope, and every expectation spiraling through the air. I open my eyes just in time to see the football pass through the hole. Something inside me lifts, then cracks. I pick up another football and throw again, sending it straight through the hole. Tears actually prick my eyes. I throw pass after pass, the way I once had. Almost every attempt hitting the target. I wipe my eyes after the bin is empty. "Yes!" I scream as loud as I can. The heaviness I've been carrying around the past few months now seems like nothing more than a weightless cloud. It feels like I just won a war.

I walk back into my house like I'm on air. My mother is standing at the kitchen counter. Her eyes are bright and brimming with tears, she must have been watching. She hugs me. "Kam, I want you to know, whether you play football or not, I love you. I never thought to tell you that because I thought you already knew. But now I'm making it perfectly clear. I'm proud of you for who you are, not for what you can do."

I hug her tighter. "Thanks, Mom." I adore this woman. I don't know what I would do without her. Oh, right, laundry, according to Laney.

My mom lets go and holds my face in her hands. "I love you." She reaffirms.

"I love you, too," I respond, and she releases me. "I gotta get to school."

"Picking up Laney?" my mom asks slyly as she opens the refrigerator.

"Yup," I smirk, and walk out of the room.

LANEY AND I DRIVE to school quietly while Justin Timberlake sings about it not being a bad thing to fall in love. At the moment, I'm inclined to agree. I squeeze her hand and glance over at the city girl whose presence, when we first met, felt like sudden impact. And still does in a way.

I pull into the packed parking lot where everyone is hanging out, not sweating first period. It's the last week of school and the vibe is laid back. Finals are done, sports are over, and summer break is about to begin. You can feel the excitement in the air.

"Ready for your last week as a high school student?" Laney smiles at me.

I look at the brick building I've spent the last four years in. Lots of memories, lots of fun, some regrets.

"Yeah, I think I am," I smile back.

Laney opens the door, but I snatch her hand. "One thing, though."

"Oh? What's that?"

I reach into the back seat. "I want you to wear this." I hold up the shirt. Laney looks down at my practice jersey and then back up at me. "I know it, and you know it, now I want everyone else to know exactly whom you belong to."

She beams as she pulls on the jersey. It goes perfect with her little cut-off shorts and Converse sneakers. I wonder if one of these days I can persuade her to wear a pair of cowboy boots. Preferably naked.

"I think it's only fair if I wear something of yours, you should wear something of mine."

I look at her funny.

"Relax. It's not my underwear or anything." She giggles, as she removes a thick, black, braided bracelet from her wrist. I would have never even noticed it; she's wearing like twenty of them. "I made it for you."

"You did?" I slip it on. It feels right.

"Mmmm-hmmm. I wanted you to have something to remember me by."

My face falls. "Are you going somewhere?"

"Maybe. I still haven't decided where to go to college."

"What are your options?" I swallow the lump in my throat. I know Laney has never been thrilled to live here, even if she did say the country was growing on her.

"New York, New Jersey, Maryland, and Alabama."

"Alabama?" My interest is piqued.

"Yes. Miranda talked me into applying to the University of Alabama. She has this nutty hope we could go to college together."

"And you're having trouble deciding?"

"I'm not sure the new star quarterback for the Crimson Tide wants his high school girlfriend toting after him all year." She bites her lip. It's sweet and sexy all at the same time.

"Laney? Are you crazy? I'm personally driving to Tuscaloosa so you can drop off your deposit." I pull her

over the seat and into my arms. Then I kiss her so hard she squeaks. I hope everyone sees, too.

"So, you wouldn't mind if I stayed?" She bats her eyelashes. A piece of dyed red hair is falling over her face.

"Mind? Lemon, if you decided to go anywhere else, I would haul you back here. No questions, no arguments."

Laney kisses me, and there's so much heat behind it, the windows may just shatter. "Keep that up, sugar, and we may end up in the storage room." I joke.

"One, don't ever call me sugar. Two, I think we still have twenty minutes before first period." Laney smiles shamelessly.

"I love you." I laugh.

Laney freezes. Her blue eyes, wide. Whoops . . . that just slipped out. I wait for a response. And wait and wait. Should I worry yet? Then Laney relaxes in my arms and slips her hands around my neck. "I love you, too."

A string of words have never sounded so good. Except for 'you have been accepted to the University of Alabama.'

"Let's go, Lemon. I want to show my new bracelet off." I smack her ass.

She kisses my neck.

We each step out of my pickup and meet at the back of the cab. I grab her hand and look up; that's when I notice everyone staring. Laney fidgets.

"Why are you fidgeting? I thought you were used to being in the spotlight?"

"I never said I was used to it." Laney squeezes my hand. "I'd rather it be reserved for the men in my life," she whispers.

"Well, that better change fast. Because if they didn't know you before, they sure as hell are going to know you now." I grin down at her.

Lucky number seven: Kamdyn Fucking Ellis's girl.

ONE NORTHERN MORNING

Alabama's golden boy has everything he's ever wanted.

He's smashed the school record for most passing yards, touchdown passes and completed passes during his college career. He is the winner of the Maxwell Award as the Nation's best all-around player, and is slated to enter the NFL draft. But even with all his success, he was unable to hold onto the one thing that was most important to him-Laney Summers.

Laney and Kam have long since gone their separate ways, but one Friday morning sports broadcasting class and an unforeseen threat to Kam's brightly shining future has these two back on a very familiar path. A path full of love and lust and unresolved feelings. A path where life-altering decisions have to be made, and questions need to be answered—like what's more important your heart or your career?

In life, as in football, you won't go far unless you know where the goalposts are.

~Arnold H. Glasow

PROLOGUE

LANEY
Winter Break, Freshman Year

HE DIDN'T SHOW UP...

I'm standing across from a camera crew in my father's newly opened restaurant in our hometown. You know, the one he moved us to my senior year of high school—Nowhere, Alabama. It's a full-service diner with a modern twist on down-home cooking. I know he's my dad and all, and I'm supposed to brag, but the food really is amazing. Especially the wildly flavored milkshakes. My favorite, the frozen hot chocolate. It reminds me of New York when he would take me to Serendipity on a Sunday afternoon. Those were the best times. I didn't realize how much I missed them until he started concocting his own recipe and using me as his guinea pig taste tester.

The cooking channel isn't here to feature Celebrity Chef Riley's new eating establishment, though. No, they're here doing a segment on master chefs and their children. Which means I'm on camera right now. *Me.* I *hate* the spotlight, but I want to support my father. So, over the last several hours, with bright lights shining in my face, I've assisted as he made our favorite meal—the one I would demand as a child. Spaghetti and meatballs.

Kam was supposed to be here. He knew how important this was to me—he knew how nervous I was—and he promised. He's been doing that to me a lot lately—making promises and never following through. I know he doesn't do it on purpose. At least, I keep telling myself that.

He's a pretty popular person, at the moment. He led Alabama to the conference finals, and then won. *As a freshman.* That's almost unheard of, unless you're Kamdyn Ellis.

He's a natural born star.

And my absent boyfriend.

I watch, trying to hide the disappointment, as my father presents a plate of perfectly coiled spaghetti with meatballs and happily garnishes it with a sprig of parsley. When he's finished, he wraps one arm around my shoulders and smiles into the camera.

"And there you have it. Spaghetti and meatballs a la Laney and Riley Summers," he says in this watered-down Southern accent.

"Thanks for joining us. May your plates be full and your company be plentiful." He throws in his signature catch phrase—the one he became known for on the cooking competition that made him famous. It's something similar to what my grandmother used to say when we would sit down for holiday meals. Food and family, she firmly believed, are two staples that go perfectly together.

"And cut," the director yells with a huge grin. "Perfect." He shakes my father's hand zealously. "You two were great. Great chemistry. Laney, you're a natural."

"Thank you." *I think.* There didn't feel anything natural about being filmed for three hours. But if he liked it, that's all that matters.

"Hungry, kiddo? I promised the crew some dinner when we wrapped up."

"No. I'm good, Dad." I wrap my arms around myself. My stomach is in knots, and my chest is aching. *He didn't show up.* "Maybe a milkshake later."

"You got it." He knocks my chin with his fist, lightly, lovingly. He knows something's wrong.

A second later, the bells of the diner jingle as Kam comes barreling through the front door. "Did I miss it?"

I stare at him silently over the counter. "You missed it." I try to keep my emotions in check, but I am so fed up.

"Shit. Laney, I'm so sorry." He starts his spiel. "My agent called last minute. A reporter wanted an interview. It was only supposed to take a few minutes—"

"I got it, Kam," I interrupt him curtly.

"Lemon . . ." He coos my nickname remorsefully. I'm not mad. I'm just hurt, and Kam's apologies just aren't cutting it anymore. No matter how sincere.

"No more apologies." I shake my head sorrowfully. "Why don't we just call this what it is."

"What's that?" Kam's baby blues flash with concern.

"Quits."

"This is not quits, Lemon." He's stern.

"I can't do this anymore." My voice is small. So small, I barely recognize it. So hurt, I can barely stand it.

"Come on, this was just a hiccup." He tries to argue, maybe reason. Either way, I've made my mind up.

"It's a hiccup that's going to keep happening for the rest of your life. I know who you are, and I would never want to change that. But I have competed for attention most of my life. With my mom and my dad, and now you. I'm tired of vying," I stress. "I would like to be put first, just once."

I'm not trying to sound like a whiny two-year-old, but that's just the reality of my life. I don't feel unloved. I know my parents love me. But my mom takes 'career driven' to another level. I barely ever see her, and it's been that way for as long as I can remember. When my father's career picked up, it became the same way. He was constantly working, or filming, or cooking. And now that Kam is in the spotlight and the center of attention, it's happening with him, too. I get it, but I'm starting to resent him, and I hate that. Because I love him, truly, with all my heart. But I love myself, too. It's going to tear us apart, eventually, so I'm just trying to make the split amicable. For all our sakes, especially his mother and my father, since they began dating shortly after Kam and I got together. Apparently, there was some leftover attraction from high school. You could almost see the sparks fly.

"Laney, you are the most important person in my life." The sincerity in his voice nearly has me reconsidering. Then his phone rings, ruining the moment. "Shit," he mutters, as he looks at the screen. He's conflicted about picking it up or continuing with this conversation. I know who's calling him. It's Sam the Magic Man, his agent, who calls him every freaking five seconds lately.

"Go ahead, pick it up. Talk to him. I know you have to." It's part of the game. Kam is going to the NFL, and this is part of the path to get there.

"Lemon, this isn't over," he says strictly, the phone ringing in his hand.

"Yes, it is." I start to walk away.

"Lemon!" Kam raises his voice as I disappear into the kitchen. "Lemon!" The phone annoyingly rings again. "Lemon! Damn it! Hello." I hear him snap just before the door swings closed behind me.

Chapter ONE

KAM
*Three Years Later
Spring Semester, Senior Year*

I BREATHE IN THE spring air as I walk across campus. It's early morning. Well, relatively. Being up at eight-thirty is hellish for most college students, but normal for me. I've already worked out, eaten breakfast, showered, and dressed. It's just part of my routine—the routine I've followed since I stepped foot on this university three and a half years ago.

I walk into the communications building and find room 202. I stop short when I see the last face I ever expected to see sitting in the third row, playing on her phone. Her hair is pulled up into a tight bun with a few tiny red streaks standing out against the deep dark brown. She's wearing cutoff shorts, a black T-shirt, and white Converse. The sight of her actually makes my heart palpitate. It still stings when I think about the day we broke up. *"Let's call this what it is . . . quits."*

I never quit.

I walk up and quietly slide into the desk next to her. "Well, well,

well . . ." Laney looks up with just her eyes when she recognizes my voice. I think she's just as thrown as I am. "What is an architect major doing in an eight-thirty a.m. sports broadcasting class? On a Friday, no less?"

She huffs and puffs as she cocks her head to look at me. "I needed a one-credit class, and this was the only one I could fit into my schedule."

"Uh-huh. Sure it wasn't because you just wanted to see me?" I purposely tease her.

"I can assure you, it wasn't. If I wanted to see you, all I'd have to do is pick up the school newspaper, or go to their website, or turn on ESPN."

"None of those things compare to being seen in the flesh." I smile brazenly.

"Nope, you're right about that." She points to my neck.

"What?" I place my hand on the skin.

"Bite mark."

"Oh." I chuckle.

"Same old Kam," she remarks as the professor writes his name on the whiteboard in front of us. He's very young, maybe mid-thirties, but dressed like a twenty-something frat boy—plaid polo, cargo shorts, and flip-flops. This class is going to be cake.

I sneak glances at Laney as we go over the syllabus. She looks older, more mature, but some attributes are still exactly the same—long silky legs, a plump, pouty mouth, and a perky rack. She's still sexy as hell and as tempting as sin.

I try not to think about how her exotic perfume affects me as the professor glosses over each bullet point. It seems like he's more eager for this class to be over than the students are.

At the forty-five minute mark, he calls it.

"Next week, have chapters one through three read and prepare to participate. Dismissed."

I walk next to Laney as we slowly exit the room. "Partners for the final project?" I ask her.

She shrugs, considering. "Sure, why not. We can just report on you."

"An interview?" I beam.

"I know how much you like to hear yourself talk," she digs lightly.

"Wear a skirt for the Q&A. I like legs, too," I banter back.

"Kam!" She smacks me on the stomach just as a guy with glasses and both hands gripping the straps of his backpack walks up to us. He doesn't look happy.

"Hey." He snakes his arm around Laney's waist possessively and stares me down. *Is this guy for real?*

"Hey." She smiles up at him. "Steve, this is Kam."

"Yeah, I know who he is. Mr. Big Shot Quarterback," he says, standoffish. He has an accent sort of like Laney's. He's definitely not from around here. "Ready to get out of here, Lay?"

"Lay?" I curl my lip. That's the worst nickname ever.

Steve glares. I just eye him up like the dufus he is. Is she seriously with this guy?

"See you next week, Kam." Laney sighs melodramatically.

I lean forward, encroaching on her personal space just to fuck with *Steve*. "Later, Lemon," I rasp, winking arrogantly, then walk away.

LANEY

FUCKING. KAM.

He would stroll into the only, one-credit BS class I have ever taken. If it wasn't for a four-credit independent study I took last semester, my credits wouldn't be all messed up, and I wouldn't have had to sign up for *sports broadcasting* on *Friday freaking morning*. Now, I get to spend the next three months with Kam and his inflated ego—*and his gorgeous eyes and sexy mouth and arsenal of southern charm.*

"Laney?" Steve says my name flatly.

"Huh?" I look up from my coffee cup.

"Daydreaming about your ex?"

"What?" I respond defensively. "Of course not." *Liar!*

"Did you know he was in that class?"

"I had no idea. Although, now that I think about it, Kam *is* a communications major."

"Appropriate, seeing how he didn't have a problem communicating with you."

"Yeah, well, that's Kam. He's never had a problem communicating with women."

"Just as long as he doesn't try to communicate too closely, we won't have any issues."

I actually laugh. Steve's green-eyed monster doesn't rear its ugly head often. But don't let the glasses and bookworm exterior fool you. He definitely has a hothead side. It's sort of what I like about him. He's intelligent, good-looking, and just alpha enough without going overboard. He's also from New York, which is part of the reason why we work so well. We understand each other. Speak the same language. Being with him feels like a little piece of home in the middle of Alabama.

After Kam and I split, we didn't speak for almost a year. But it's sort of difficult to avoid the son of your father's very serious girlfriend, especially when he's sitting across the dining room table from you during the holidays. Breaking up with Kam was the hardest thing I ever had to do, but nearly four years later, I know it was the right decision. He's in such high demand. Everyone wants a piece of him. He's constantly traveling with the team, or doing interviews, or charity appearances, or being invited to elite parties . . . the list goes on and on. There's no time, in my opinion, for a serious relationship or commitment of any kind. Kam needed his freedom, and I loved him enough to give it to him. I needed someone I could have a solid foundation with, and Steve gives me that.

"Stop. You sound jealous and insecure." I roll my eyes. Kam and I are older news than Jennifer and Brad.

"I call it intuitive." He corrects me, as he takes a sip of his latte. "You know his reputation."

"I know Kam's reputation all too well. But I think I'm immune from his prowling. Been there, done that. If you know what I mean."

Steve grimaces. "Did you have to provide a visual?"

"I think you were just looking for an excuse to picture me naked."

"Naked with *me*, maybe."

"I can make that happen, you know," I purr, slumped casually in my chair.

Steve smiles wickedly. "Well, what the hell are we waiting for?"

"To finish our coffee?" I respond coquettishly.

Chapter THREE

KAM

I PUSH THROUGH ONE more set of Fire Hydrants.

Squeezing the dumbbell to my hamstring behind my knee, I raise it up as high as it can go. I pause for a few seconds in that position, and then lower my knee back down. Wondering why a quarterback is doing leg lifts? Because it takes more than a strong arm to throw with precision and accuracy. It's an entire body synchronicity, from legs to torso to chest. Fire Hydrants strengthen my outer hips, which also aids in *precision* and *accuracy* for *other* physical activities, if you know what I mean.

A guy's gotta blow off steam, *somehow*.

My phone rings on my last rep. I lower my knee to steady myself and answer on the third ring. "Yo."

"How's my number one?" It's Sam, my agent, and he sounds overly enthusiastic.

"Keeping in shape." I wipe the sweat off my face with a hand towel and take a swig of Gatorade.

"That's what I like to hear. That's what *NFL scouts* like to hear."

"Is there a reason for this phone call? Or do you just miss me?" I mess with him. Sam has been my agent since my freshman year. He's one of the best in the business and practically poached me from every other agent who showed the slightest bit of interest after I won the conference finals. He's become as much of a friend as he is a pain in the ass. He has a big, flashy, LA personality, and the talk to go with it. They don't call him Sam the Magic Man for nothing.

"I've heard rumors."

"What kind of rumors?" I take another swig of Gatorade.

"You're going to be the first pick, first round, at the draft."

I nearly spit out the blue liquid. "What?"

"Yup. Seattle wants you, bad. They know you're going to get snatched up quick with New York, Denver, and North Carolina all in desperate need of a quarterback."

"But Seattle has the best starting quarterback in the league. Why would they go for me?"

"Because they want to keep it that way. You're a threat, Kam. You're destined to be great, and everyone knows it. Their mentality is keep your friends close and your enemies closer, if you know what I mean."

"I know what you mean," I answer slowly, contemplating what going to Seattle could mean for my career. Not much playing time my first year.

"I'll keep you posted on the details. This stays hush hush."

"Understood."

"Good. Later, All-Star." Click.

The draft is in two months. Two short months and everything I ever worked for, fought for, will finally come to fruition.

The BIG DREAM may finally come true.

I WALK UP TO class to find Laney and Steve talking by the door. I take it upon myself to interrupt their conversation by squirming between them to get into the room. Why? Because I can.

"Lemon." I wink at Laney and completely ignore *Steve*.

"Kam," she echoes my name only slightly bothered. Steve, on the other hand, seethes under his breath.

"I'll see you later," I hear Laney tell him as she follows me into class.

It's been several weeks and I still can't figure out what the hell she sees in him.

He seems like a big fat jerk-off to me.

I want to know if she and *Steve* are really serious, but that just seems too personal to ask. It would make it seem as if I'm more interested than I have any business to be. Laney and I are friends and Lord knows it took us years to get to this point. Our breakup was bad—it was ugly, it was emotional, and very messy. But after it was all over, I learned one thing; being just friends is way better than not having her in my life at all.

At least that's what I keep telling myself. *Just friends is better than nothing. Just friends is better than nothing...*

"Did you draft the questions, Lemon?" I ask to distract myself.

"Right here." She pulls out a piece of paper from her notebook and waves it in the air. We decided to do a mock interview. Her as the reporter and me, well, the sports star. How perfect. This project has A written all over it. I take the sheet from her and gloss over the questions. They are all pretty straightforward, nothing I haven't answered before. Then my eyes suddenly land on the second-to-last question and stay glued there.

Do you have any regrets?

My throat actually closes. I'm not one to believe in regrets. You lose, you mess up, you move forward. It's how you survive under the immense pressure. No living in the past. But as much as I walk around like Superman, I'm human just like everyone else, and I have weaknesses, too. I will always regret losing Laney. I will always regret not fighting harder to keep her. I will always regret that, in the end, football really was more important.

"These look good." I hand her back the paper rigidly.

"Good." She smiles at me. "I was going to try and get some studio time later this afternoon so we can record it. What do you think?"

I nod silently. "Sounds like a plan. I'm free."

"Perfect." She looks at me funny. "You okay?"

"Fine." I plaster on a fake smile. I get to spend more time with you . . . as just . . . *friends*. . . .

LANEY AND I SIT in the tiny studio setting up the microphones and recording equipment.

"How did a *non*-communications major book studio time last minute in the middle of the semester? You usually need to reserve it weeks in advance."

Laney smiles cunningly. "I bribed Josh. It is amazing what a signed football from Kamdyn Ellis can do." She opens her bag and pulls out a brand-new football.

"You didn't?"

"I totally did." She tosses me the ball. "He's a huge fan. We had a class together last semester and all he did was gush about you." She theatrically rolls her eyes. "I could have thrown up, but knowing how much he loves you worked in our favor. We didn't have to wait weeks to record this interview. It's one more thing I can cross off my to-do list."

"You are devious, Lemon."

"I know. He wants you to sign it to my one true love."

I snort. "Like hell."

Laney nearly falls over laughing. "To my biggest fan?"

I curl my lip. "Too cliché."

"Fine then, just think of something before we leave."

"Will do. Are we ready?" I straighten in my chair.

"We are." Laney takes a seat next to me and adjusts the small microphone on the table in the recording room. As part of our final project, we needed to show we could not only conduct a broadcast or interview, but edit it, as well.

Laney starts the interview by introducing herself and me. Then she fires away.

What is your favorite thing about football? What does your workout schedule look like? How did it feel to lead your team to the conference championships and win your freshman year?

As I said, all questions I have answered a million times, and probably will answer a million more. But as she ticks off each one, my anxiety rises a little more because I know what's coming. I know which question is going to test my composure.

"Mr. Ellis, do you have any regrets?" Laney looks dead into my eyes.

I inhale a few deep breaths before I answer. "Personally or professionally?"

Laney's face falls as an air of silence blankets the room, suffocating it with tension. "Both," she responds.

I never take my eyes off her as I answer. "I don't have any professional regrets. Every triumph and failure has led me to where I am now. I just want to keep moving in the right direction. As for personal regrets? I think everyone has those. I lost someone I loved once, and I will always regret that," I admit, as stone-faced as possible.

Laney just continues to stare; the tense silence becoming almost unbearable.

"Sometimes . . . she regrets it, too." She clears her throat and looks away. I nearly fall out of my chair. Did she just admit she misses me?

"Mr. Ellis, thank you for the candid honesty." She moves on. "I have one last question before we end." Laney tucks some hair behind her ear. I want to reach out and touch her, but I don't. I keep my distance, my heart fluttering from her confession.

I nod her on.

"Where do you see yourself in five years?"

I smile. I know exactly where I see myself. "Playing for the NFL with a Super Bowl ring on my finger."

Laney chuckles. "I have no doubt, Mr. Ellis, that one day that will become a reality."

With that, Laney ends the interview.

"Please don't forget to sign the football and give it to Josh." Laney gathers her notebook and pen and places them into her book bag.

"I'll drop it off right after I leave."

"Thanks." She slings her backpack over her shoulder. "Good interview. You're a pro." She teases me, but I'm not in a very playful mood.

"You weren't so bad yourself." I grab her hand as she walks by.

There's regret on her face, but she doesn't pull away. "Whatever it is you think you need to say, you don't. It's in the past. We've both moved on."

I stare, wondering if she really believes that. I sure as hell don't. She feels as real today as she did three and a half years ago.

"I really am sorry," I profess, rubbing my thumb over her hand.

"Don't be." She pulls it away and touches my face; my skin nearly catches fire.

I'll always be sorry.

"I gotta go. See you next week, All-Star."

My chest tightens from the term of endearment. She hasn't called me that in years.

"Same time, same place," I assure her wistfully.

Laney throws me a sweet smile over her shoulder right before she leaves. I don't follow. Instead, I sit back down and spin the football mindlessly on the table. Some strange sense of hope tingling inside me.

"I lost someone I loved once, and I will always regret that."

"Sometimes . . . she regrets it, too."

Chapter FOUR

LANEY

"DO YOUR HOMEWORK, LEMON?" Kam drops his notebook on the desk next to me and slips casually into the seat.

"Yes, you?"

"Right here." He pulls out a typed page and waves it in my face.

"Am I supposed to be impressed or something?"

"Or something," he flirts.

Kam has been doing that a lot lately. Flirting. With me. I don't know if it's the end of the school year high, the fact we're graduating, or what, but the last two and a half months, spending every Friday morning together, has done something anomalous to our estranged relationship. We have two official classes left before we take our final and then head out into the world. Me to New York to start an internship at a prestigious architectural design firm, and Kam to the NFL. Both our career dreams seem to be coming true.

"What's with the pigtails, Lemon?" He flips my hair flirtatiously with his pen.

"Nothing." I shrug him off. "Can't a girl wear pigtails?"

"She can." He eyes me hungrily. That look is so dangerous.

"You know what pigtails are good for?" he leans in and whispers.

"What?" I raise an eyebrow speculatively.

"Pulling." He yanks on my hair a little harder than just teasing. I actually clench my thighs. Maybe I'm not so immune to Kam's prowling after all.

Professor Katz begins class, and Kam and I both shift in our seats. But it doesn't matter how much I try to concentrate on what the teacher is saying; the only thing I am aware of is Kam. I can feel him looking at me. No. Not just looking—licking me with his eyes and tangling me in an uncomfortable excitement. A precarious predicament. Kam is off-limits in so many ways. We've been down this road before, and as much as our physical chemistry is off the charts, there are too many old emotions attached. I couldn't open that door again, not even for one, carefree, no-strings-attached night. *One, uninhibited, reckless, pulse-pounding night.* I can almost feel the way he used to touch me. The light caresses and strong grip, when our bodies would fuse together and the world would disappear. It was the only time I really ever had Kam—the only time I received his undivided attention and unconditional love. There's a sudden ache in my chest as I find myself mourning what we once had.

"Laney?" Kam shakes me by the shoulder. "Are you alright?" I look over at him and then around the room. We're the only two left.

"Fine." I clear my throat.

"You were in some pretty deep thought."

"I guess I was." I scan over Kam's facial features. His big baby-blue eyes, strong jawline, and prominent nose. Tack on his charismatic personality and southern charm, and he's the epitome of quarterback playboy. He hasn't even been officially drafted yet, but he's going to take the NFL by storm. I predict it already. He's Alabama's golden boy, and he'll be the National Football League's, too.

To me, however, he'll always be the man I let go.

I move to stand, extinguishing all the feelings flaring inside me like wildfire.

"Do you want to grab some coffee?" Kam asks as he walks me out. "Or is your attack dog waiting for you?"

I laugh. "No. Not today."

"So how 'bout it? Coffee? I'll even buy you a muffin."

"I can buy my own muffin. And coffee, for that matter."

"So, is that a yes?" he asks hopefully.

I contemplate for a second; my good sense flying right out the window. "Sure, why not?"

We grab a table outside at the nearby coffee shop on campus. It's a warm April morning, and the humidity is comfortably low.

"So . . ." Kam says with a smirk.

"So . . . ?" I reply with the coffee cup in front of my mouth, concealing my mirroring expression.

"In a few more weeks, this will all be a distant memory." He motions to campus.

"Yup," I agree, cheerfully. "Are you nervous about the draft?"

"A little," he admits reluctantly. "Everything I've ever wanted is right at my fingertips."

"That should make you happy."

"I am happy."

"You sure? Because you sound like something is missing."

Kam stares at me stoically, ticking his jaw. "Not something. Someone."

I freeze mid-sip. I'm not even going to ask whom because the way he's looking at me tells me everything I need to know.

"Kam." I sigh.

"Laney."

"Don't do this," I beg.

"Why?"

"Because."

"That's not a reason."

"It's complicated."

"What's complicated?" He leans over the table. "Tell me you don't have any kind of feelings left for me. Tell me that spending time together over the last few months hasn't changed anything."

"It hasn't." I assert.

"Why? Because of that idiot you date?"

"Kam, that's enough." I stand up, and he follows suit, blocking me before I can pass.

"You can't be serious about him, Laney." Kam glares down at me. His big, blue eyes sparkling in the sun.

"I am serious about him." I hold my ground.

"Why? What does he have to offer you?"

"That's a loaded question, Kam. Are you sure you want to hear the answer?"

"Yes."

I huff. "Steven has never broken a promise. Or not shown up when he said he was going to. He doesn't spend half our relationship apologizing for the things he didn't do. He may not be you, but at least I know I can rely on him."

Kam's expression darkens. He wanted answers, and I gave them to him.

"You can rely on me, Laney."

"Not the way I need." I shake my head, attempting to move around him, but he places his hand firmly on my hip. My heart stops.

I look up into his eyes pleadingly. We can't do this; it's just going to be heartbreak all over again.

He opens his mouth to respond, but his phone interrupts him. *Some things never change.* Kam lets it ring three times before he hesitantly removes his hand and answers it.

"Yeah." He never takes his eyes off me. "What's up, Sam?"

That's my cue. I bypass his rigid body and make a beeline straight to my car.

Same shit, different day.

KAM

COFFEE DID NOT GO how I expected.

Laney just hightailed it out of here, and Sam is barking in my ear about something on the news.

"Find the closest television and turn on the local news!"

I walk into the coffee shop and ask the girl behind the counter if she can switch the channel. She recognizes me immediately and blushes.

"Absolutely," she drawls.

As soon as she changes the channel, my face is plastered on the screen with the headline: "Alabama Golden Boy Accused of Sexual Assault."

What. The. Flying. Fuck?

Chapter SIX

LANEY

IT'S STARTING TO RAIN.

After the coffee debacle with Kam, I came home, changed into the crumpled-up shirt I slept in last night, and disappeared under the covers. I listened to the large droplets hitting the pavement outside like a drum until I fell asleep.

I don't know how long I have been holed up, but when I throw the covers off, I realize its dark outside. I just lie there as the thunder pounds and my emotions stir. I have been in a state of conflict all day. Wanting Kam is one thing, but knowing he wants me back is entirely another. It opens doors that should stay closed forever. Dangerous, emotional, heated doors that warn *Enter At Your Own Risk*. And loving Kam has always been a risk.

I know I have to stop obsessing. About Kam, about the past, about the present, and about the very potent feelings that just won't seem to go away. *I'm going to drive myself nuts!*

My personal-crisis situation calls for some pizza and ice

cream . . . stat.

I shoot out of bed and walk into my living room, and what do I see as soon as I look at the television? Kam's face.

"You're up." Steven is lounging on the couch holding the remote.

"How long have you been here?" I ask him, peeling my attention away from the headline for only a second.

"A few hours. We were supposed to grab dinner, but you were asleep when I got here. Are you feeling okay?"

"Not really. What's going on?" I point at the television.

Steven snickers. "He's not so golden after all."

I want to slap him for his scathing remark.

"Why are you always hating on Kam?" I snap at him. "Does he intimidate you that much?"

Steven stands up. "He doesn't intimidate me, Laney. I've just always seen him for what he is. And now the rest of the world sees it, too." He motions to the screen.

Alabama Golden Boy Accused of Sexual Assault.

"Kam would never do that," I immediately defend him.

"You sure?"

"Positive."

"I guess you would know," he replies snidely.

"What exactly are you accusing me of?"

"Still having feelings for your ex," he says blatantly. "The two of you have been pretty cozy lately."

"We're friends."

"Is that what you're calling it?"

"You're being an idiot." *Just like Kam called you today.* "Where is this coming from?"

"It's coming from the fact I'm not blind, and that you wear his practice jersey to bed every night." He pokes me in the chest. I look down and realize I'm wearing the dark-blue jersey with the number seven, a pair of underwear, and nothing else.

Steven heads for the door. "Why don't you call me when you work out what the hell you want. Although, I'm pretty sure I already know what that is." Thunder booms and lightning strikes just as he storms out, slamming the door behind him.

I stand there gaping. *What the fuck just happened?*

First Kam, now Steven? My life is turning into a car wreck.

I rub my temples, sit on the couch, and turn up the volume so I can listen to the news report that's playing on a loop. "*Sandra Collins, twenty-two, has accused the football phenom of raping her at a college party after she repeatedly refused his advances. An investigation is underway.*"

I just shake my head, disbelieving. Kam may be many things, but a rapist is definitely not one of them.

I suddenly jump from a knock at the door and a simultaneous lightning strike that illuminates the whole room. I run to answer it, fully expecting Steven to be on the other side, gearing up for round two. Instead, I swing it open to a soaking wet, hooded figure.

"Kam?" I yank him inside. He's drenched from head to toe.

"I'm sorry, I didn't know where else to go." He pulls off his hood and unzips his sweatshirt. His wet T-shirt is clinging to all the right places, most notably his chiseled chest and ripped abs. I look away so I don't start salivating.

"It's fine. Come in." I walk him into the living room of my moderate-sized, off-campus apartment. "How did you get here?"

"I walked."

"In the rain?" my voice elevates.

"I had to get away. There are reporters crawling all over my house. I snuck out the back."

Kam shares a spacious colonial with three of his teammates. It's a hub for parties and a hangout for almost every athlete on campus. "I'm sure you've heard by now." He shivers, dripping wet in the middle of my living room.

"I just saw," I reply as I grab a towel from the bathroom and hand it to him.

"Thanks."

"No problem," I respond sympathetically.

"Fucking, bullshit," he mutters as he wipes his face, then sneezes. Not good.

"Um, not to sound like I'm coming on to you, but you should really get out of those wet clothes before you catch your death." Kam's grim expression lightens a little.

"Lemon, if you wanted to see me naked, all you had to do was ask."

"Kam, please." I stop him right there.

"Just sayin'." He shrugs.

I roll my eyes. "I can put your clothes in the dryer, if you'd like. If not, don't sit on my couch until you're dry." I walk over and plop down on the plush sofa.

"You're tougher than nails, Lemon." He shrugs off his sweatshirt, then peals his T-shirt off right in the middle of the room.

"What the hell are you doing?" My mouth actually goes dry. *Holy Roll Tide.* College football does a body good.

"Talking my wet clothes off so I can sit down."

"I didn't ask for a strip show. Use the bathroom!" I point.

"Sorry. Didn't think it would be a big deal. It's nothing you haven't seen before." He turns toward the bathroom door, his back muscles rippling as he walks. I sink into the cushion. Good lord. I actually fan myself. It's been nearly four years and the man still has a panty-melting effect.

Dangerous, emotional, heated door that warns Enter At Your Own Risk.

Kam comes out of the bathroom wearing nothing but the towel I gave him. "Where's the dryer?"

I motion to a set of doors off the kitchen. I think I have lost the ability to speak. Kam, naked, in my apartment. How did we suddenly get here?

He pops his clothes into the dryer with a tight grip on the towel. Once they're tumbling, he takes a quiet seat next to me on the couch. It isn't very big, but it's comfortable. With his head hanging low and elbows resting on his knees, he looks over at me. And that's when I see it. The devastation. He may have been playing around before, but he can't suppress what he's truly feeling.

"You okay?" I ask considerately.

He shakes his head, and a few renegade droplets fall from the ends of his disheveled hair.

"Did you assault that girl?" I have to ask, even though I already know the answer. I just have to hear it from his own mouth.

"No," he asserts. "I don't even think I know her."

"Then why would she accuse you of such a thing?"

Kam shrugs. "A payout, maybe? I wouldn't be the first athlete it's happened to."

"Despicable."

"Whatever the reason, it's destroying my reputation." He scrubs his face with his hands. "Which, in turn, is destroying my career."

"Her accusation doesn't affect the way you play football," I argue.

"No, but reputation is everything when you're being drafted. No one wants to recruit a bad seed."

"Anyone who knows you knows that you would never hurt or disrespect a woman. And if you don't get drafted because some stupid girl looking for attention cried rape, the NFL needs to seriously re-examine itself."

Kam smiles wearily. "Thanks, Laney." He puts his hand on my bare knee and heat races across my skin. "How is it every time my career is in jeopardy, you always know the right thing to say?"

"I'm a genius." I laugh nervously.

Kam laughs, too, pushing my knee playfully. He's so cute when he's just Kam. Not Mr. All-Star or Mr. Popularity. Just Kam. We stare quietly at each other for a long while. The energy in the room heavy, suppressive almost.

Dangerous, emotional, heated door that warns Enter At Your Own Risk.

"It's getting late. You should probably get some rest." I move to stand, but he snatches my wrist.

"Can you stay with me?"

I crease my eyebrows. "Kam, I don't think—"

"Come on, Laney. This is probably the worst day of my life. I don't want to be alone." He looks at me with raw emotion.

I know it took a lot for Kam to admit that. And he must really be hurting if his defenses are down.

"Okay." I give in. How can I say no to such a bleeding plea? "Lie down."

Kam situates himself on the three-cushioned couch so I can slide up next to him. I rest my head on his chest as he wraps both arms around me. He smells like rain. We're scrunched pretty tightly, but somehow we make it work. We lie there just listening to the storm. Thunder cracking and lightning brightening the room every now and again.

After a while, I start to drift off, warm and secure in Kam's embrace.

"Hey, Lemon," Kam says just before I fall asleep.

"Yeah?" I murmur.

"Nice shirt."

KAM

THE RELENTLESS BUZZING WAKES me up.

"Shut it off," Laney mumbles sleepily, swiping at my face.

"It's across the room." I snuggle up next to her in an attempt to go back to sleep. I'm too comfortable to move. The buzzing eventually stops, and I drift back to sleep.

It then starts again. Shit.

"Kam," Laney whines, and I finally give in. It's annoying the crap out of me, too.

"Fuck, okay." I clumsily uncurl myself from her body. It's not exactly easy to maneuver in just a towel, but I eventually make my way off the couch without flashing her and swipe my phone from the top of the washing machine. I groan. Fifty missed calls and umpteen text messages. A majority of them from Sam, some from my parents, and a few from my coach. As I hold the phone, it rings again. 'SAM THE MAGIC MAN' flashes across the screen. I growl, aggravated. I just don't want to deal.

"Sam?" Laney asks sprawled out on the couch. I have to take a few deep breaths. She looks beyond edible wearing only my practice jersey. I can't believe after all this time she still has it, let alone wears it. It was a pleasant surprise when she opened the door last night. I honestly didn't know where else to go, and I knew Laney would be the one person who wouldn't hound me. She'd make me feel like a normal person. She always has. She never was caught up in the celebrity, or the status, or the juggernaut that is 'Kamdyn Ellis.' She's always just seen me.

"The one and only." I make my way back to her.

"What are you going to do?" She pulls her legs up so I can sit, and I catch a peek of her skimpy boy shorts when she shifts. What I wouldn't give to just lose myself in her body for a few hours. The way I used to.

"Kam?" She pulls me from my daydream.

"*Going* to do?" I answer distracted. "I have no idea. I know what I would *like* to do."

"And what's that?" Laney sits up straight. Her long, dark hair is messy and tangled; it looks like we spent the night doing more than just sleeping. *I wish.*

"Disappear."

"So, why don't you? Maybe some time to yourself will be good for you."

"I don't want to be alone," I say unwaveringly.

She stares at me as if she knows exactly what I'm getting at. Her big, blue eyes twinkling. I want to disappear—*with her.*

"We could go to your father's cabin by the lake. It's remote," she suggests without skipping a beat.

"We could do that." The use of the word *we* makes me feel lightheaded. Laney and I spent a bunch of weekends up there the summer we were together. Both with and *without* my father. "You're okay with getting out of here?" I want to make sure this is what she wants and it's not just some pity party for me.

"I'm good." She grins. "I could use a change of scenery."

"What about *Steve?*" I ask.

"I don't think Steven will care. He broke up with me last night."

"Sorry." I tell her. *Not really.* Really, I'm fucking elated she got rid of that Yankee idiot.

"Don't be." She sighs. "I didn't see a future with him anyway."

I shoot her a shit-eating grin.

"Don't even go there."

I can't help it. "Told you so."

"Put a sock in it, All-Star," she says sourly. "If we're going, let's go."

"Decision made." I try to sound upbeat, but worry, doubt, and fear are slowly oozing through the cracks of my resolve. I don't want to lose my entire career—everything I worked for, my lifelong dream—because of some stupid bullshit that never even happened. I rein in my anger and focus on Laney's face. If anyone can ground me, it's her.

"Let's get dressed." She nudges me with her foot, then stands. I just follow her with my eyes. Does she know how grateful I am? Do I even have the courage to tell her?

"Thank you." I clear my throat as she hovers over me, her bare thighs right at eye level.

"What are friends for?" She smiles, then disappears into her bedroom.

Friends . . . ?

#ALABAMAALLSTARASSAULT IS TRENDING ON Twitter. My life as I know it is over.

"Give me that." Laney snatches the phone from my hand. "We are disappearing, remember? That means no phones or computers or Twitter or Facebook."

"How shall we ever survive?" I jest, glumly.

"We'll eat, drink, and be merry," she says dryly as she turns on her car. It's a little, red, sporty thing with two doors. Definitely not conducive for a six-foot-three college athlete. My knees are practically touching my chest. "There's a reason it's called comfort food." She pulls out of the parking lot.

"I don't think much is going to comfort me," I say as we drive past my house. I pull my hood over my face and slouch down as she speeds by. There is still an entourage of reporters camped out on the large front lawn.

"Vultures," Laney spits.

"Appropriate comparison," I add disheartened.

It takes two and a half hours to get to the cabin, but we need to stop for food and supplies if we are going to disappear comfortably. About an hour and a half into the drive, Laney pulls up to a food store. She knows it's the closest grocery chain for miles.

I feel some apprehension when we walk into the busy market. I don't want anyone to recognize me. And luckily, no one seems to take notice of us as we start to stroll the aisles.

"What do you want to eat? What will make you feel *comforted*?" Laney jokes.

I grin. What a loaded question that is. *You—stripped naked in the freezer aisle.*

"Um . . ." I keep my dirty thoughts to myself. "What's that sandwich your dad used to make?"

"Which one?" she asks as she throws a couple bags of chips into the cart.

"The one with the cheese and the sauce he used to bake."

"Oh, Reuben."

"Yeah. That one." I snap my fingers.

"Okay, I'll grab the ingredients and some other stuff for lunch and dinner. I'll stock up just in case we are missing for a few days. Can you grab another cart and get drinks?"

"Sure." Missing for a few days with Laney? *Yes, please.*

We meet up at the checkout aisle. She has a cart full of food that looks like it will last us a few months, not days. And I have enough Gatorade to hydrate an elephant. I grabbed Laney a few bottles of Snapple Iced Tea because I know she likes that brand. No southern sweet tea for this girl.

I will never understand.

Once the groceries are loaded into the car, we make the last leg of our trip to the cabin. It's midday by the time we get there. The house is nothing extravagant, but it sits right on the lake and has a killer view. There's even a boat dock. I couldn't tell you how many nights Laney and I hung out on those wooden planks just talking and gazing at the stars.

"Well, you wanted to disappear. This is definitely as close as it gets," Laney remarks as I open the front door. The inside décor still has my mother's touch. Flower-patterned furniture and plush throw rugs over the hardwood floor. In the divorce, my mother got the house I grew up in and my father got the lake house. He doesn't come here often—I think the last time was Fourth of July last year. The town puts on a huge fireworks display over the lake that's pretty impressive.

"Okay." Laney slaps my back. "You grab the bags, and I'll start lunch."

"I can do that." It takes me three trips to bring in all the food bags. By the third trip, Laney is practically done with prepping lunch.

"You're fast."

"I'm hungry." She pops a piece of lunchmeat into her mouth.

"How come I only like the Reuben sandwich that your father makes?" I grab a piece of meat for myself. "I've tried them a few times, and they're never quite the same."

"Because he uses pastrami instead of corned beef, Russian dressing instead of Thousand Island, and muenster instead of Swiss."

"Is that it?" Intrigued, I eat another piece of pastrami.

"Yup." The oven beeps.

"Ten minutes and lunch is served." Laney picks up the sandwiches she constructed on a baking sheet and pops them in the oven. She washes her hands and then comes to lean against the counter next to me, staring at the oven. *Now what?*

There's some heavy-duty silence as the seconds tick by. I watch her as she watches the oven.

"What are you looking at?" she asks with an uncomfortable smirk.

"Nothing. You . . . I guess."

"Why?" She glances over at me.

I can't help it. I have to ask. "Were you wearing anything besides panties under my jersey last night?"

"It's *my* jersey," she corrects me. "And why do you care?"

"Because I'm curious." I smile. "Do you wear it often?"

Laney fights not to look at me again. "I wear it often enough."

I turn toward her. Our bodies an inch away from each other. "Do you think about me when you wear it?" I probe.

"Think about you how?" She turns her head and wets her lips. My blood simmers.

"You tell me?" I lean in closer; her sweet scent and seductive mouth have a magnetic effect.

It takes Laney an eternity to answer, trapping us in this oppressive stare.

"I never stopped thinking about you," she admits, timidly. The one thing I have always loved about Laney is her self-confidence. She's tenacious, and independent, and assertive, but what never fails to make me crumble is her honest vulnerability. I've only seen her expose that side to one other person—her father. So, I feel privileged when she's brave enough to open up to me.

"I never stopped thinking about you, either," I more than willingly divulge. I don't even give her a chance to process my response as I grab her by the neck and smother her with a hot, hungry kiss. A kiss I have been suppressing since the moment I laid eyes on her at the beginning of the semester.

In true Laney fashion, she doesn't back down or try to break the connection. Instead, she opens up to me almost like a flower waking up to the sun.

She moans as I grope her body, putting my hands wherever I damn well please. Wherever they are yearning to touch. A blast of possessiveness shoots through me as we tear at each other's clothes. There's no rhyme or reason at the moment, just blinding passion and insatiable want. I rip her T-shirt as I yank it off her, exposing her perky little breasts and silky skin. Like I've never touched a woman before, I attack her neck and fondle her over her bra. It's a little, black, lacy thing I'm positive she wore just to drive me crazy. Speaking of teasing, I skim my fingers along the lace, yanking it down to free one nipple. I twist and roll it relentlessly until Laney is clawing at my back, begging for more.

I assail her mouth, trapping her face with my hands until neither of us can breathe.

"Kam, Jesus." She pants, grinding against me.

"I need you, Laney. I need you so bad." I am beyond desperate.

She nods frantically with her eyes closed and cheeks flushed. It's all the agreement I warrant. I lift her right off the floor and plant her on the countertop. Crushing my lips against hers, I struggle with one hand to remove her shorts. Once off, she moves to unbutton my fly—rip it open is more like it. I barely have time to grab my wallet out of my back pocket before she is yanking my jeans and underwear all the way down my thighs. I'm tingling from head to toe with need as I hastily remove a condom and sheath myself with it. There's one lingering moment before I take her that resonates through the whole house. One heated heartbeat of yearning that passes between us before I grab her and sink into the most euphoric tightness I have ever known.

Pure. Ecstasy.

"Kam," Laney sighs with a firm grip on the back of my neck.

That one word sends me soaring. My name spilling irrepressibly from her lips.

"God . . ." I grind out, unable to control the urges streaming through

my system. It doesn't matter how long we've been apart or how many other women I've been with; no one makes me feel the way Laney does. Nothing compares to her scent, or her skin, or her sighs.

"I want you to come." I grip her hair and let loose. "I'm dying to feel it. It's been too long."

"Kam—" She rolls her hips and draws me closer as I thrust as deep as I possibly can, over and over until it happens, until her muscles spasm and she lets out a strangled moan, delivering exactly what I demanded. Her uninhibited pleasure. Her climax slingshots me straight to the edge, the buildup almost catastrophic. I lift her off the counter and pin her against the refrigerator, sprinting after my own abandoned pleasure.

With Laney's arms and legs wrapped tightly around me, I lose control. I let go of all the stressors and come violently, as if this climax was locked away for three and a half years and only Laney could set it free.

I moan feebly into her neck as my leg muscles tremble. I'm completely sapped.

Laney kisses my temple and runs her fingers through my hair until I look up at her. I have so many things I want to say, but I can't seem to articulate any of them. Before I even have a chance to try to communicate what I'm feeling, an ear-piercing sound rocks us back to reality.

"Lunch!" Laney exclaims as she tries to wiggle out of my hold.

"Shit!" I set her on her feet and grab for the oven mitts as the sound of the fire alarm shreds our eardrums. I pull out the burnt Reubens as Laney opens the front door and windows.

The alarm stops after I wave a mitt in front of it while trying to pull my pants up at the same time. Once everything settles down, I look over at Laney. She's wearing my T-shirt in place of the one I destroyed, and a big fat smile. She then erupts in laughter. It is kind of funny.

"At least we know the fire alarm works," she says as she slips her arms around me.

"It most definitely does." I embrace her, kissing her head.

LANEY

I SLEPT WITH KAM.

I knew it was inevitable. I knew what I was doing when I suggested coming to the cabin, but I couldn't resist him anymore. I barreled straight through the forbidden door, and there's no going back now.

I clean up after lunch, throwing the paper plates away and wiping the counter. The first batch of Reubens went into the garbage, obviously. The second batch was made with no interruptions. Thank God. I needed a breather. I needed to process everything that just happened, and I knew one sexual advance from Kam and we would be in the same predicament all over again. I feel hyperaware of everything now, as if my body flipped a switch and Kam is the electricity running through my veins.

"Hey, Laney," Kam comes bounding down the stairs. "Look what I found." He smiles brightly flipping a football in the air.

"The extension to your hand?" I ask flippantly.

He chuckles. "How's your arm, Lemon?"

"Rusty," I admit as I throw the sponge back in the sink.

"Well, let's see what we can do about that." He spanks me on the ass arrogantly as he walks by and straight out the front door.

I follow him outside, and for a few, wistful moments, I watch as he palms the ball expertly with a look of elation on his face. Kam personifies the term 'love of football.'

"C'mon, Lemon!" He tosses the ball to me while I stand on the front porch of the house. "Let's have a catch."

"I haven't thrown a football in a long time," I inform him, walking down the stairs holding the ball.

"That's okay. You had a great teacher." He grins shamelessly. "It's as easy as riding a bike."

"Says the professional quarterback." I flip the football around, re-acquainting myself with the leather.

"I'm not pro yet." Kam puts is hands on his hips. His T-shirt pulling tightly across his chest, outlining the sculpted muscles. The same muscles that were just pressed up against me. That body makes me forget how to freakin' think.

"Soon enough." I place my fingers between the laces, the way Kam taught me, and launch the ball at him. It actually spirals pretty nicely, but my aim could use a little work. He needed to take a step to the side in order to catch it.

"Not bad, Lemon. Not bad at all." He smiles brightly as he throws it back. His spiral is way prettier than mine.

"Maybe it is like riding a bike." We lob the ball back and forth. I lost count how many times Kam and I did this when we were together. Just hung out and watched the sunset over the lake while throwing the football around. It was so simple, yet meant everything.

"Lots of things we used to do are just like riding a bike," he insinuates.

I catch the ball then flutter my eyes. But I can't deny he's right. Our chemistry is still off the charts, maybe even hotter now than it was before. I actually get butterflies in my stomach just thinking about it. Thinking about how he touched me, and kissed and completely overtook me.

I fire the football back at him.

"Geez, Laney." He catches it in the crook of his arm. "That one had some power behind it."

I actually giggle like a little girl. What the fuck is wrong with me? The control Kam has over my panties is ridiculous.

"So, do you have any idea what team is going to draft you?" It's time to change the subject to something safer. Something that will let me hold on to my self-respect a little while longer.

"There are rumors Seattle is going to draft me."

"Seattle? Wow. They're a really good team."

"Yup."

"That doesn't surprise me."

"Why?"

"Because you're a really good player. The best player. Why wouldn't they want you?"

"Because they already have the best quarterback in the league." He sighs.

"So, what does that mean?"

"It means no playing time for me."

"Oh?" I frown, catching the ball.

"Yeah, second string sucks."

"Well, maybe you'll get scooped up by someone else first. They can't be the only team interested in you."

"They aren't, but they have first pick. So, if they want me, then that's where I'll end up."

"Too bad the draft doesn't work the other way around." I throw the football then roll my shoulder. It's starting to hurt.

"Too bad." He laughs, tossing it back.

"Well . . ." I rest the football against my thigh. "If you do end up in Seattle, just make sure to buy a parka and lots of umbrellas," I joke.

"Anything else you recommend before I'm exiled to the state with the highest suicide rate?"

"Yeah." I laugh. "A trade."

"Smartass." Kam rushes me and I try to run. But he's too fast and tackles before I make it two feet.

"Kam!" I squeal as he takes me down to the ground.

"What?" He pins me beneath him.

"Quarterbacks aren't supposed to tackle."

"In special circumstances they can."

"And you interpreted me just standing there minding my own business as a special circumstance?"

"In those little shorts holding a football? Yeah." He leans in and kisses me. I swear I melt; my body just softens right underneath his.

We don't do anything but kiss. Kam's hands keeping a firm grip on my wrists as his tongue goes exploring. He's not aggressive or overbearing, but there's enough force to make me succumb. To make me surrender and revel in the warmth of his mouth. I yank my wrists free just so I can wrap my arms around him. Just so I can get a little bit closer. We lie on the ground kissing, caressing, and stroking until we are panting and the sunlight is fading away.

"Kam," I murmur, nearly ripping off his shirt. I don't care that we're outside on the bare ground. I don't care that we have no blanket and there are owls hooting in the trees above us. The only thing I care about it is getting closer to Kam. As close as we were in the kitchen. As close as humanly possible.

"We have to go inside, Lemon."

"Why?" I suck on his neck and grind against him.

"Because . . . oh, shit, Laney." He grabs my hip and squeezes firmly.

"We've had sex under the stars before." I try to persuade him.

"We also had protection."

"I'm on the pill," I hastily reply.

Kam pauses, looking down at me dumbfounded. "No condom?"

"Only if you're hell-bent on using one. Then I understand."

"You trust me that much?"

I simply nod. "I shouldn't?"

"You definitely should." He hauls me up. "But if we're going raw, I don't want it to be some two-cent fuck in the dirt."

"Oh? That doesn't sound so bad to me."

"Lemon," Kam scoffs amused. "We can roll around in the mud tomorrow. Tonight, I want dinner, then dessert, and then you."

"In that exact order?" I rub up against him.

He inhales a collective breath. "Yes."

"Fine." I can hold out if he can.

I think.

"Good." He smiles boldly. "Now get in the kitchen and start cooking, woman."

"What!" My voice elevates three octaves as Kam takes off toward the house, laughing. *"You better run!"*

I SPOON A SERVING of lemon chicken onto each of our plates and have chocolate chip cookies baking in the oven. Kam said he wanted dinner and dessert before me, so I'm giving him exactly what he asked for—while wearing nothing but one of his T-shirts. No bra, no panties, no nothing. He's watched me cook like a starving animal for the last hour, and I know he's craving more than just food. We both are.

I place the plates on the small kitchen table and go to take a seat when Kam tugs on my arm. "Where are you going?"

"Um, to sit." I point at my chair.

He shakes his head. "You sit with me." He pulls me onto his lap. This is hazardous on so many levels, but I love it. Kam cuts up all the chicken and asparagus on his plate, then proceeds to start feeding me and himself, alternating forkfuls of food back and forth between the two of us. The simple dinner I expected has turned into something flirtatious and playful.

"Kam." I giggle as he teases me with the food, pulling the fork back just as I go to take a bite. He's getting way too much enjoyment out of seeing me squirm.

The timer dings on the oven, alerting me the cookies are done. If he wants to tease, then I can tease.

I slip on the oven mitts and bend over provocatively as I pull the cookie sheet out, giving him an eyeful while he sits at the table.

"Shit, Lemon," I hear him mutter. I smile to myself. By the time I place the cookies on the stove and remove the heat-resistant gloves, Kam has me by the waist with his face buried in the nape of my neck.

"I think I'm done with dinner."

"What about dessert?"

"You are dessert." He spins me around and kisses me forcefully. I have no problem being dessert, especially if Kam is the one indulging in me. "Bedroom, now." He starts to back me out of the kitchen.

"Your celebrity status has made you very bossy," I quip.

"It has nothing to do with my celebrity status," he says between eager kisses.

"What does it have to do with, then?" I ask as he pushes me down onto the mattress.

"The fact that I want every inch of your body all to myself. Right. Now." He pulls off his T-shirt and I nearly expire. I know we had sex already, and it was, well, words can barely describe it. But it was so fast and furious, I didn't get a chance to take him all in. Now that we are taking our time, relatively, I get to appreciate one of my favorite things about Kam—*his abs*. And all I can say is holy mother. Kam has always had an incredible body—tall, lean, and muscled—but the person standing in front of me now is a transformed man. He's double the size he was in high school, his shoulders are broader, his arms are bigger, and his stomach is shredded. I think I might be drooling.

"Like what you see, Lemon?" Kam asks as he crawls on top of me completely naked.

How do I answer without my voice cracking?

I nod zealously.

"Good, because I like what I see, too." He yanks my T-shirt up and over my head.

I hand myself over to Kam as he explores my body with his mouth. He takes his time tracing the curves of my hips and the dip of my stomach. I know there should be foreplay, and I'm all for taking whatever pleasure Kam has to give me, but right now, this second, I just want him. I couldn't be more aroused or more ready.

"Kam," I plead as he licks my neck and massages my breast. "Please."

"Please, what?" he rasps.

"Please . . . I just want you." I slip my hand between his legs and rub his erection. God, I sound so needy, but I'm dying to be with him. Plain and simple.

"You know all you have to do is ask," he groans, nestling himself between my legs. "Or beg. I don't mind begging either."

"This isn't a time for jokes." I wrap my legs around him as he rocks against me; the feeling of skin on skin is indescribable.

"Who's joking?" He sinks inside me, and my body and mind nearly split in two.

"Shit." I arch underneath him, trying to get as close as physically possible.

"Fuck, I know, you feel so good." He surges his hips and traps me in his arms. The sensations passing between us are all-consuming, and soon we're caught up in an unstoppable cadence of longing, hunger, and desire.

As I get closer to the breaking point, I pop my eyes open to find Kam watching me. His lustful, hooded gaze is so poignant; a lump of emotion gets caught in my throat.

"You are so fucking amazing, Laney." He thrusts harder, deeper.

"How did I ever let you go?"

I feel tears threaten as my arousal tingles in my core. "You weren't the only one who let go." I hold on tighter, burying my face in his neck as my breathing quickens and I find my release. For those few, short, enrapturing seconds, I belong solely to Kam and regret every moment we ever spent apart.

I'm left quivering in his arms as he stills inside me, his fevered skin matching the temperature of my own.

I'm feeling way too many things at once; too many conflicting emotions all battling to take control. The loudest and most pronounced? Love. The love that's always been there. It almost breaks my heart.

I close my eyes and breathe in Kam's masculine scent. I don't want to think about what tomorrow has in store for us. Tonight, I just want to pretend the different directions our lives are heading in, aren't going to inevitably tear us apart.

KAM

LANEY IS THE ONE person who can make me forget.

She's the one person who can make me feel normal.

She's the one person I never want to let go of again.

The last three days have been surreal. Not that the situation is ideal, but being isolated with her has made me realize just how important she is to me. Just how important it is to have her in my life. Sex whenever—and however—I want it doesn't suck either.

She's always been bold, but she has most definitely come into her own. Lucky me.

It's early Monday morning, and the house smells like pancakes. I had offered to cook, but Laney insisted. So, at the moment, I'm leaning against the doorframe watching her stir batter with her dark hair in a messy bun, wearing only my practice jersey and a pair of knee socks. A man could get used to this.

If I'm being honest, he already is.

With no restraint, I walk up behind her as she sets the bowl down on the counter. It doesn't matter that we made love all night and once this morning. My appetite seems insatiable when it comes to Laney. I press her back to my front and tilt her face up so I can deliver a kiss so hot it could fry bacon.

She moans into my mouth and softens against me. When we separate, I keep my hand on her throat and stare down into her twinkling blue eyes. "What's my name?" I ask her.

"Kam," she replies with an impish smirk.

"What's my full name?" I press.

"Kamdyn," she says, the insinuation in her tone is unmistakable. She belongs to me.

"That's right, baby." I toy with her. "Kamdyn. Fucking. Ellis." I steal another kiss, running my hand down the center of her torso. This shirt isn't going to be covering her body much longer. I wonder how she'll feel about cooking naked?

Just as my wild thoughts tear free, we hear a car door slam outside.

Laney's eyes widen as I release her and look out the window.

"What the . . . ?" I hurry outside to greet Sam, who is decked out to the nines in an expensive suit, dark sunglasses, and large, gold, pinky rings.

"What the hell are you doing here?" The surprise is evident in my voice. He's supposed to be in LA.

"I've been trying to get a hold of you for the past twenty-four hours," his deep, baritone voice rumbles.

"Oh, I shut my phone off," I explain. "Trying to steer clear of all the craziness."

Sam slides his glasses down his nose and gazes at the house. "Mmm-hmm. Is that what you call it?"

I turn to see Laney leaning against the doorframe watching us. She doesn't look happy.

"Yes, that is what I call it." I address Sam sternly. Laney and Sam have never been fond of each other, and I want to avoid making either of them uncomfortable. "What are you doing here, anyway?" I cut to the chase.

"Well, since you fell off the face of the freaking Earth, I had to come retrieve you in person and deliver the news." He pushes his glasses back up his nose, concealing his black eyes.

"What news?"

"The charges have been dropped."

"*WHAT!*" I nearly jump out of my skin. "How? Why?"

"When the police investigated your accuser, they found a shrine to you in her dorm room. Seems she was your number-one stalker."

"You're joking?" I almost feel sick.

"Afraid not. Welcome to stardom, kid. Additionally, when they examined her, there was no evidence of rape. From what I have gathered, the girl was mentally unstable and not taking her medication."

"So, she's sick?"

"Yes."

"That's sad."

"Yes, sad and fucking infuriating because she almost wrecked your career before it even began," Sam says, exasperated. I get he's upset. I'm upset, too, but I'm glad it's over, and I actually feel sorry for that girl. Mental illness is a disease; I just hope she gets back on track and doesn't do this to anyone else.

"So, you came all the way from LA to tell me this?"

"Yes, and to set up a press conference. We need to polish your image, and an interview at your high school is a great way to make you look good. The place will be packed with people just trying to get a glimpse of their hometown hero."

"When is that scheduled for?"

"Three hours, so we need to scoot."

"Three hours?" I look back at Laney; she hasn't moved from the doorway.

"Shit." I rub the back of my neck. "Okay. Let me get my stuff together."

"By stuff, do you mean Laney?"

I glare at Sam. "I mean my clothes and shit."

"Um-hmm," he reverberates. "You two back together?"

I don't take my hard look off Sam. "Yes. You have a problem with that?"

"Nope. I didn't then, and I don't now. Laney is good people. I just don't want you distracted, that's all. And females can be one hell of a distraction, especially when they look like that."

I glance back at Laney—she's sexy as hell without even trying. Even Sam sees it. "I'll be right back."

Laney disappears into the house as I walk up the front porch and through the door.

"Everything worked out?" she asks, wringing her hands together.

"Surprisingly, yes." I smile as I approach her. "All the charges have been dropped, and my name is clear."

"Good. I'm glad." She sighs, weakly.

"Me, too." When I try to touch her, she backs away. So not good. "Laney, what's wrong? Is Sam being here making you uncomfortable? I know you don't like him . . ."

"I like Sam just fine," she interrupts me, returning to stir the pancake batter.

"Sure you do, about as much as you like sweet tea." Her lips curve up faintly. "We have to get back. Sam's set up a press conference. I have to make a statement and . . ."

"Go then," she interjects, clearly upset. I'm upset, too; I wasn't ready to leave so abruptly. But reality calls, and I have to be there.

"I want you to come with me." I pull the bowl out of her hands and entwine her fingers with mine, imploring her to look at me.

"I can't."

"Why not?"

"You know why, Kam." Her grip tightens as she looks directly at me.

"I honestly don't." I search her face. What the hell is she talking about?

"Nothing has changed."

"What do you mean nothing's changed?" I drop her hands. "Everything's changed."

"No, it hasn't. You still have your life, and I still have mine."

"What the hell does that mean?" It feels like rocks are being piled in the pit of my stomach. "The last three days didn't mean anything?"

"Of course, they did—"

"Or did you just want one last fuck with Alabama's most eligible bachelor?" I snap. "Is that it?"

"Of course not!" She takes a step toward me.

My chest feels like it's caving in. "I can't believe you are pulling this shit again, Laney."

"Kam." Her voices wavers.

"Don't." I fight not to flip out. "I trusted you."

"Kam . . ." she pleads, but I am so over this bullshit.

"Forget it." I brush past her. Sam was right—women are nothing but a distraction. I walk out on her, leaving all my stuff behind.

I haul ass to Sam's massive black pickup, climb in, and try to ignore the gaping hole in my heart Laney just ripped open.

"Where's your girl? We waiting for her?" Sam asks.

"She's not my girl," I spit. "Just drive."

Sam pauses, staring at me for a beat, before he throws the car into D and speeds away.

I watch the house get smaller and smaller in the sideview mirror, right along with the happiness I allowed myself to have for thirty-six, short hours.

Chapter TEN

LANEY

I PERMIT THE TEARS to fall only after the truck disappears.

When it's safe. When I know Kam will never see them. I clean up the kitchen, pack our stuff, and lock up the house. I'm completely numb. I will never forget the distraught look on Kam's face before he stormed out. *I trusted you.* Those words are like a butcher knife hacking me apart. I never meant to hurt him. I never meant for him to feel like he couldn't trust me. But what I said was true. He has his life and I have mine. He's slated to go to Seattle, and I'm moving to New York. How would we ever make that work?

I knew the inevitable would happen; I just didn't think it would be so soon.

Without even thinking, I drive to the one place I know I'll find solace.

"Sugar pie." My father beams when he sees me walk through the front door of his diner. "What are you doing here?" He put his arms around me, and I surrender in his embrace, fighting back tears.

"I was with Kam . . . at the cabin."

"Oh?" His face perks up.

"With the allegations and media hounding him, he needed to get away. So, we went to his father's cabin. To hide out."

"I see." My father eyes me speculatively. "I didn't realize you and Kam were *socializing* again."

I turn red. What can I say? Don't worry; nothing happened? We'd both know that'd be a lie.

"We were *reconnecting*." I clear my throat.

"It doesn't look like it went so well."

"It was going fine until *Sam the Magic Man* showed up," I say spitefully. "And reality came crashing down on us."

"Yeah. It does have a habit of doing that." His southern twang surfaces with a vengeance. "Where is Kam now?"

"At a press conference. Sam set it up at the high school."

"Why didn't you go?" He walks me over to the counter and urges me to sit down on one of the stools.

"I figured he'd be surrounded by enough people. His adoring fans, the press, *Sam*."

"Ah, Sam, your favorite person in the whole world."

"Most favorite," I respond sarcastically. Kam was right—I do like Sam as much as I like sweet tea.

"Well, what are you gonna do?"

"About what?"

"About Kam."

"What's there to do? You don't give up everything you worked toward for some guy. All your hopes, all your dreams."

"You're right. Some guy? No. Kam, maybe."

"Dad." My jaw drops. Is he being serious? He knows what I had to go through to get that internship. How unbelievably hard I had to work. Architecture is a highly competitive business. If you don't get in with the right firm, you might as well give up before you even start if you want any kind of a halfway-decent career.

"Laney, look." He puts his hands up in surrender. "I'm not trying to tell you not to go after your dreams, or give up who you are. I'm the last person who would ever suggest that. But, in hindsight, I realize your mother and I made a lot of bad decisions. We worked against each other instead of with each other. Maybe you and Kam just need to find a happy medium."

"I don't think that exists unless I go where he goes."

"Would that be such a bad thing?"

"Possibly." I chew my lip. "I don't want to lose myself because of his career. I don't want to feel like I'm always second."

"I understand, sugar. Living a public life is trying, but if I know one thing, Kam would never put you second. Yes, he has obligations and responsibilities, but the love is there. That's what's important. And trust me, he needs you."

"For what?" I scoff. "He has the world at his feet. He practically walks on water."

My father smiles knowingly. "Kam may be surrounded by adoring fans and hounding media, but believe me, he really is alone."

"Are you speaking from experience, Daddy?"

"Possibly." He smirks. "You were always my rock, maybe it's time to be Kam's."

I gaze into my father's kind eyes. I honestly never thought of it like that. Kam walks around with an air of authority that feels untouchable. Sometimes you almost forget that he's human.

Was I wrong to leave him the first time? My heart says yes, but my head says no. Now that I look back, maybe I was just a confused, eighteen-year-old girl trying to adjust to college and jealous she had to share her boyfriend with the whole damn world.

"Looks like you've got some thinking to do." My father smiles sympathetically.

"I sure do," I pout.

KAM

I'M SITTING IN THE middle of Radio City Music Hall surrounded by my peers. As I look around, the excitement and stress is almost palpable. This is the biggest day of my life. My dream come true. Draft day.

There's a rumble of voices as the crowd anxiously awaits the picks to begin. We've only been sitting a short while, but it feels like days have passed. This moment will define the rest of my life; it will shape my career and my future. I've never felt so nervous; my stomach is actually flip-flopping, my palms are sweaty, and I'm a little lightheaded. I was calmer during the Sugar Bowl when we were down by six and the entire game was riding on me. I catch sight of the commissioner walking purposefully across the stage that is plastered with the NFL logo and insignia. As he takes his place behind the podium, cameras flash and a wave of quiet blankets the room.

My whole body starts to prickle as he leans forward and speaks into the microphone. The moment leading up to the first-round pick announcement is electrifying. It feels as if I am balancing on a razor-sharp tip three hundred and fifty feet in the air.

"With the first pick in the two thousand fifteen NFL draft . . ." The commissioner pauses for effect and the room seems to tilt, or maybe that's just me, "Seattle selects . . . Kamdyn Ellis, Quarterback, Alabama."

The crowd erupts into a deafening roar as time stands still. Congratulations pour over me. My mom is crying, my dad is beaming, and Sam's eyes are sparkling like chocolate diamonds. Everyone I love is here, except one very important person.

I walk onto the stage a split man. It is the happiest day of my life and the most disappointing. Every time I pictured this moment, Laney was always a part of it. Even when we weren't together she was still somehow here. I have regretted walking out on her every second. Regretted not fighting harder to keep her. Just like before. History has a way of repeating itself.

Looking back on it now, I should have just flung her over my shoulder when she started with that crap and not given her a choice in the matter. She should be here, with me, right now. She should be sharing the spotlight because she is the other half of my happiness. That's my life—one part football and one part Laney. I have always known that, and I'm not going to stop until I put the two broken pieces back together again.

I smile as I pose for pictures holding up the navy and white jersey. It doesn't feel real, at least not yet. It has to sink in that I am now a professional football player.

My dream come true.

I meet Sam backstage as the commissioner continues to announce names.

"My man! My man!" Sam clasps both of my shoulders and squeezes hard. "I knew it! I knew you were gold the moment I laid eyes on you. That's how you succeed—hard work, dedication, and *me*." He smiles obnoxiously.

"Modest, as always," I jibe.

"Only one person gonna toot your own horn in this world, and that person is yourself."

"You've done just fine tooting my horn for me," I point out.

"That's just because I know this business and how to make it to the top. That's why they call me Sam the Magic Man. I make things happen."

"You can do anything that needs to be done." I repeat the mantra I've heard a thousand times.

"Smart and pretty." He smacks my face playfully.

I smile connivingly. "I need some magic, Sam."

"What kind of magic?" He creases his eyebrows.

"I need a Sam special. I need something to get done..."

Several weeks later . . .

I CRACK MY KNUCKLES nervously as I stand in front of the door. *Just knock already.*

I inhale a deep breath and rap firmly on the wood. I wait a few, impatient seconds then knock again.

"Hang on!" Someone yells before the door swings open. Standing on the other side is a guy who doesn't look much older than me, wearing a bathrobe over his clothes and a five o'clock shadow. I eye him up and down. *Who the hell is this clown?*

"Yeah? Can I help you with something?" His eyes are glassy and his speech is slow.

"I'm looking for Laney Summers."

"Who?"

"Laney Summers," I repeat. "She supposedly lives here." *Her father gave me this address.*

The guy pouts his lip and shakes his head. "Never heard of her. No one but me and Jarvis live here. Just moved in."

I peer into the apartment and see a bunch of boxes on the floor, a couch you couldn't pay me to sit on, and a fat, orange cat.

"Sorry," I tell him, confused and disappointed. "I didn't mean to bother you. I have the wrong address, apparently."

"No problem, man." He takes a good hard look at me. "Do I know you from somewhere?"

"Doubt it." I start to step away.

"Yeah, I do." He snaps his fingers as his bloodshot eyes light up. "You're . . . You're Kamdyn Ellis. Quarterback for Alabama and first-round draft pick!"

Shit.

I rub the back of my neck. "Yup, that would be me," I admit reluctantly.

"Holy shit!" The guy nearly back flips out of his bathrobe. He's awake now. "Hold on! Hold on!" He trips over his own feet as he runs back into his apartment. "Please, man, would you sign this?" He holds out a black Sharpie and a football.

"Sure." I take the items and sign away. "What's your name?"

"Nick." He pipes up with a dopey smile. His expression makes me smile.

To Nick, nice bathrobe. Kamdyn Ellis

I hand him back the football, and he reads my note. He beams. "It's my favorite. I've watched every single one of your games in it. Brings luck."

"Good to know." I laugh. "Huge fan of plaid." *Not really.*

"Sorry I can't help you find who you are looking for. Might want to ask the landlord to see if she left a forwarding address."

"I'll do that." I nod. "Nice to meet you, *Nick.*"

"Awesome to meet you," he replies like a kid in a candy store.

I turn to leave as he shuts the door. Before I try the landlord, I pull my phone out on the way to the elevator, search my contacts and find the one number I haven't dared to dial in weeks. I press send and hold my breath. Someone answers after a few rings.

"Hello?"

"Lemon . . . ?"

Chapter TWELVE

LANEY

"KAM?"

"Where are you?" he asks immediately.

I look around the airport and pause. Does he know I'm here? "I'm . . . in Seattle."

"You're *where?*" He sounds flabbergasted. Maybe he doesn't know I'm here.

"Seattle," I say again. "I was going to surprise you. I gave up the internship. I want to try, Kam," I divulge nervously. I had planned to do this in person, but since he has me on the phone, I might as well spill all my secrets while I have the nerve. "I'm sorry. For everything."

"Laney." He breathes, and it sounds pained. I instantly regret every decision I've made over the last few weeks. I walk over to the nearest restaurant to get out of the way of the bustling travelers. When I look up at the television, I see Kam's name flash across the screen.

In an unforeseen turn of events, Kamdyen Ellis, Alabama all-star and first-round draft pick has been traded to New York. In a statement released earlier today by the team, the organization could not be happier to have picked up Ellis and are ecstatic to start the phenom in the upcoming season.

If someone brushed by me at this very moment, I would surely fall over.

"Kam?" My voice is shaky. "Where are *you?*" I am ninety-nine percent sure of the answer, but I just have to hear him say it.

"New York."

I almost sob.

"I wasn't letting you go again, Laney. Not without a fight, this time."

"Oh, my God." I turn straight around and head back to the gate I just deplaned from. "I'm coming back." I push against the crowd moving in the opposite direction as me. It feels like I'm wading through the ocean, but I don't care.

"I'll be at the airport waiting for you."

I wipe away the tears and giggle. "You better."

I hang up once I reach the ticket counter. "I need to go back to New York. Right now. The next flight," I tell the attendant behind the counter. Her eyes widen.

"Is everything alright, ma'am?"

"Yes," I answer excitedly. "I just need to get home, right away."

"I wasn't letting you go again, Laney. Not without a fight, this time."

She types some info into the computer. "Looks like the next flight with open seats leaves for JFK in an hour."

"I'll take it."

"Do you want to know the price of the ticket?"

"It doesn't matter." I whip out my credit card. "Book it, please."

Within a few minutes, I am booked on the flight and hurrying to the gate that is on the other side of the terminal. I make it just in time.

I buckle my seat belt between a very large man with a fedora and an overweight woman munching on french fries. If I was in any other state of mind, this flight would suck, but nothing could ruin my amazing mood. It feels like a boulder has lifted off my chest. I have ached for Kam every second we have been apart. Watching him walk away affected me in ways I couldn't explain or even comprehend. I just knew I needed to try and make things work. I needed to know if we could really have it all. So, I gave up my apartment in New York, resigned from my internship at the architecture firm, packed my bags, and headed for Seattle not knowing what the future would hold. I was hoping Kam would at least talk to me, see that I made the big gesture, and forgive me for being such an idiot. Forgive me for not trusting in us—or in him—enough to take a leap of faith. I have always been levelheaded. It's my curse. Sometimes it costs me things, like missed opportunities or the courage to take chances; it almost cost me the man I love.

But not this time. This time we are going to do things right. Kam has a bright future and major responsibilities ahead of him, and my father was right, it's time that I'm his rock.

I already know he's mine.

I AM NEARLY JUMPING out of my seat by the time the plane taxis and pulls up to the gate. I am squished all the way in the back between two people triple my size, but it doesn't stop me. As soon as we are given the green light to deplane, I jump up and start to push past the other passengers pulling down their luggage from the overhead. Some none too happy with me, but shit, that's life. *Welcome to New York.* The five-and-a-half-hour flight was torture. It felt twice as long since all I could think about was Kam. Once I finally make it through the jetway and into the airport, I literally run. Luckily, my only carry-on was a duffel bag, so it was easy to stow under the seat and sling over my shoulder. I pass the last, final exit sign and make it down the escalator to passenger pickup. It takes me all of three seconds to spot Kam. He's standing in the middle of JFK wearing loose jeans, his favorite Roll Tide T-shirt, and a backward hat. He's circled by a small crowd of fans, asking for autographs. Years ago, this would have upset me—today, I'm elated because I see how happy it makes him. He's a born star, reveling in the role. There is no denying it and no taking it away from him.

"Kam!" I yell just as I step off the escalator. He looks up at the sound of his name. My feet carry me faster than I anticipate and the crowd parts as we move toward each other. I don't even try to be modest. I drop my bag, jump into his arms, and plant a kiss right on his lips that mothers have to shield their children's eyes from. I hear the camera phones snapping away, and know this kiss is going to go viral in nanoseconds, but I couldn't care less. Right now, the only thing that's important is *Kam* and *me*. Not his status, or his fans, or the media, or even the team.

What's most important is just *Kam* and *me*. . . .

Chapter THIRTEEN

KAM

MY EYES ARE STILL closed when I feel Laney's lips on my neck. I moan sleepily.

"Morning," she sings softly, seductively.

"Morning," I grumble as I grab her hip.

"Time to wake up, sleepyhead." She grazes her hand over my shorts.

"Persuade me." I smile with my eyes still closed.

"I plan to." She covers my mouth with hers. Our tongues duel and our hands roam until there's nothing separating our bare skin. Laney spoils me. Ever since we got back together, our bond has become stronger. There are no questions, only answers: yes, mine, always, yours, together, forever.

She straddles me, taking the reins. She likes to take control, and I love it when she does. That confidence is what has always drawn me to her; it's what makes me so fucking hot for her.

She's all ready to go; no foreplay this morning. Laney knows what she wants and she's going after it. It isn't much different outside the bedroom either. She's a wildfire, a force to be reckoned with.

In one easy move, I'm engulfed in her heat, my body turning over with ecstasy. I pull her against me—one hand on her neck, the other on her lower back—and meet her thrust for thrust. This isn't going to last long, but it's going to be intense.

Fucking intense, just like Laney.

"Kam." She bites my bottom lip and moans as her body stiffens.

"Laney," I goad her as I slide my hand down to her ass and push her right to the precipice.

"Fuck!" She spasms, coming hard, which prompts my own release. I watch her until I can't keep my eyes open, until the pleasure drags me under, demanding total control.

How did my life become so perfect? It seems as if I just woke up one day and had everything I ever wanted.

"Morning," Laney says lazily, resting on my chest.

"I think you said that already." I breathe heavily.

"Did I?" She laughs. "I can't remember what happened before five minutes ago."

"I can walk you through it again if you want to be reminded," I say salaciously.

"Mmm, I would be all for that, but someone has to get up for training camp." She pushes off me, but I grab her wrist.

"If it was anything else, I would blow it off to spend the morning in bed with you."

Laney smiles, her tousled, brown hair falling over one side of her flushed face. "I know."

"Good."

"Now, get up." She jumps out of bed and drags on my T-shirt. "If we hurry, I can make coffee and we can catch the sunrise."

"I'll be out in a minute," I say, smiling like a stupid fool as she leaves the bedroom. My life really is perfect.

I take a quick shower, throw on my training clothes, and find Laney out on the balcony. Since the stadium is not technically in New York, we decided to rent an apartment in New Jersey, a stone's throw away from the city. Laney was able to get her internship back, so she takes the ferry across the Hudson every morning. I'll admit, for a small-town boy, I am enjoying the big city. I'm especially enjoying the happiness I see on Laney's face every time she takes me to one of her favorite places or shares a story from her childhood. Being here, I can picture it all.

Laney hands me my coffee as I put one arm around her. Together, we watch the morning light slowly creep up over the horizon, the buildings turning gold and orange as the entire skyline illuminates right before our very eyes.

There's definitely nothing like this in Alabama.

I draw in a serene breath, holding Laney tight.

It is one, spectacular, northern morning.

ONE PERFECT TWILIGHT

Do happy endings really exist? For Kam and Laney it looks that way. The All-star quarterback is starting for New York and leading his team to the biggest game of his career. The sassy city girl is taking strides, making a name for herself in her own career. Things look bright, but sometimes even the most sparkling relationships can lose their luster. Can Kam and Laney actually find their perfect twilight?

Chapter ONE

LANEY

SAM DRAGS ME DOWN a thunderous tunnel toward the football field. He all but kidnapped me from the comfy skybox I was happily watching the game from just minutes ago.

"Sam, what are you doing? I'm missing the last two minutes!" I tug on my arm, but his grip is like iron.

"Spoiler alert." His deep voice booms and echoes against the concrete walls. "They win."

Kam is currently playing in the NFC championship. Actually, playing isn't the correct word. Crushing the championship is more like it. New York is winning by thirty-six points. At least they were when I was so rudely plucked away from my VIP seat in the sky.

Just as we make our way to the opening of the tunnel, Sam flashes two badges at the security guard, and the behemoth man dressed in all black nods us on.

"Here." He slips the all-access badge around my neck as I'm blinded by stadium lights. The game is over, and just like Sam said, New York is the new conference champs. It's so loud and busy on the field I can barely keep my bearings as he drags me across the vibrant green turf. Confetti is raining from the heavens, massive men in padding are celebrating all around us, and the media has swarmed onto the fifty-yard line. It's not unusual for the family members of the winning team to join the players on the field after a big win, but I'm left wondering why Sam only grabbed me. As we get closer to the mob, Sam strong-arms his way through the bodies. Being an ex-defenseman himself, he knows how to break through a line. It's no secret Sam the Man and I have had our differences in the past, but we have come to a mutual understanding that we both share a special person and have his best interest at heart. Even though I question him sometimes, I've learned there's a method to his madness, and only good things have arisen for Kam from his strategy.

Speaking of the devil, once Sam and I break through the final layer of people and emerge into a little opening, we find Kam thriving in his natural habitat—the spotlight. He's in the middle of an interview, but when he sees me tucked protectively under Sam's muscular arm, he breaks out into a dazzling smile. Even after all these years, my heart and panties melt when he looks at me like that. Like I'm the only person he sees even when the entire world is watching. My cheeks heat from a combination of the superman standing before me and the embarrassment of the media spectacle. I'm not one for the public eye. That's my father's and Kam's arena. They're born celebrities while I'm just a simple city girl who loves lattes and riding the subway.

Kam reaches for me, his eyes sparkling with victory as he wraps one sweaty, dirty arm around me. He tilts my chin up and kisses me smack dab in the middle of the interview, and for a split second I wish I could hide behind the curtain of my dark hair.

It's not a chaste kiss either. It's hot, and emotive and conveys way too much for the public to see.

"Hi, Lemon," he voices in my ear so only I can hear.

Hi. I respond in my head 'cause I'm at a loss. I'm like a damn deer in headlights. That kiss was way too expressive. There's so much going on. There are too many people, and it's way too loud.

I'm dizzy.

Sam knocks Kam on the shoulder and then hands him something, but I don't catch what it is. Kam takes the object more than willingly and then looks down at me. His expression is mischievous. Those baby blues burning under the stadium lights. He starts to speak, but I can't hear a thing he's saying. I try to read his lips. I love you . . . chemistry . . . high school . . . I make out every fourth or fifth word. I start to shake. He takes my hands and then drops to one knee, my heart plummeting with him. One of the refs watching from the sidelines shoves his mic in Kam's face and turns on the volume. His voice suddenly booms all around us.

"Laney Summers," my name echoes. "I wouldn't be the man I am today without you. Your love, your loyalty, and your support are my foundation. It makes me strive to be better. To make you proud. With you by my side, I'm invincible. And I want to walk hand in hand through this crazy life with you, and only you." He pops open a little black box, and I involuntarily gasp. "Will you marry me, Lemon?"

I stare, stunned, at the huge square diamond winking back at me. Then I lift my eyes to Kam's. And in that moment, there's only us. No reporters or fans or groupies. None of the everyday chaos that being Kamdyn Ellis's girlfriend brings.

You can strip it all away—his talent, his celebrity, his status—'cause it's the man underneath who I love. The man whose heart is as vast and deep as the ocean. Whose confidence could lead an army of giants and whose character will trailblaze through history. He's a profound example of an American royal. And he's asking me to be his. Forever.

"You gonna answer the man?" Sam nudges me, and I snap out of my stunned daze.

Oh. "Of course!" I exclaim. "Yes, I'll marry you!" The happy tears fall, and I think my smile is going to actually crack my face. A roar rips through the stadium as Kam slips the ring on my finger then scoops me up into his arms. The people in our immediate circle clap and congratulate us, but all I can concentrate on is the hold Kam has on me and our image on the Jumbotron. Ellis is emblazoned across my shoulder blades. But I'm not wearing his professional jersey or even his college jersey. I'm wearing the navy-blue jersey from high school. The one that started it all. The one that told the entire student body, and the world, exactly whom I belonged to. Whom I've always belonged to, even when we were apart.

Him.

Chapter TWO

KAM

LANEY AND I HAVEN'T been farther than seven inches apart since we walked through the door. Clothes vaporized and passion ensued as soon as we were alone.

The high of the win and the accelerant of the proposal created a combustible atmosphere. It's the middle of the night, and I'm awake and alive as if it were the middle of the day. I shift on top of a naked Laney, nestling myself back between her legs.

"Jesus, Kam, again?" she moans sleepily but drops her knees, allowing me to sink into her addictive heat for the umpteenth time tonight. It never gets old being with her. Making love to her, fucking her. It's like our bodies crave each other the way they instinctually crave food and water. Being with Laney is sustenance. Nourishment impossible to live without.

"I can't help it." I move unhurriedly. "I'm wired. The adrenaline is pumping."

"That's not the only thing pumping." She cracks a joke with her eyes closed and a little smile etched on her lips.

I chuckle. "Today was the best day of my life." I kiss her collarbone and circle my hips deliberately slow. Then watch her expression morph, her beautiful facial features tightening as she bites her bottom lip. Blood pounds in my ears like the sound of a drum as I slide easily in and out of her, my cock swollen and throbbing but nowhere near ready to come. I want to feel Laney first. I want the woman I've fantasized about calling my wife since high school to fly apart beneath me. Like she does so easily. So fluidly. So in sync with my movements and body.

"Shit, Kam." She crunches up slightly, anchoring an arm around my neck. It's her telltale sign.

"Say my name, Lemon. Say my name when you fucking come."

"Kam," she huffs, knowing that's not what I want to hear.

"Are you testing me, Laney?" I drive in deep, and she emits a little gasp.

"I'm always testing you, All-star."

"Shit, if that ain't the truth." My southern drawl sneaks out as I try to keep my focus, but Laney is the one person who jumbles my concentration like the broken pieces of a jigsaw puzzle. Put a three-hundred-pound linebacker out for blood in front of me, and I wouldn't flutter an eyelash. Place a hundred-twenty-pound city girl with a sharp tongue in my path, and I fall all over myself like I have two left feet. We all have a weakness, and Laney is definitely mine. She always has been, since the moment I met her.

"Show me what you got," Laney challenges me. She knows I'll rise to the occasion. It's why I love her so much. She tests me. Keeps me on my toes. Feeds my competitiveness like a number-one contender.

"You're going to regret asking that." I thrust into her powerfully. Each strike made with precisioned purpose. "Say my name, Laney. Say it when you come. I know you're close. I see it on your face. I feel it between your legs. I know exactly what I do to you." I graze my pelvis against her sensitive clit, and she shivers.

"I'm not one of your little groupies who will give you whatever you want, whenever you want it." Fuck, this woman drives me mad in all the best possible ways.

"No, you're not." I nip at her lip as I grind my hips just a tiny bit faster. Her breathing picks up from my pace. "You're so much more than just a groupie. You're the only woman I want in my bed. The only woman I want to live inside of, and the only woman I want to hear say my fucking name."

"Fuck, Kam." She's dangerously close to the edge now.

"The whole thing, Laney." She knows what I want, and I know she wants me to force it out of her. It's a push and pull game we play.

I feed the orgasm roaring inside her. The beast belongs to me. It's all fucking mine.

With a punishing blow, the word I want to hear explodes from her lips. "Kamdyn!" She all but cries as she comes for me. The divine satisfaction I find in Laney's release is equal to the satisfaction I get from throwing a touchdown or winning a conference championship game. It's victorious, fueling the warrior inside me.

Just as her pelvic muscles loosen around my cock and her body softens I pull out and flip her onto her stomach. She's pliable from her orgasm, submitting to my abrupt change in position.

"Fuck, Lemon, you're so goddamn wet." My eyes nearly roll into the back of my head as I slip and slide through her slick pussy.

"That's what you do to me," she purrs, lifting her hips to grant me better access.

"It's what you do to me." I fuck her hard, squeezing and massaging one of her breasts as I become more intoxicated by her body by the second.

And because I am completely selfish when it comes to Laney and her pleasure, I want more. Sliding my hand from her breast to her clit, I rub relentlessly, using the wetness coating us both to demand another orgasm.

"Kam, I can't." Panting, she grabs my wrist.

"There's no such thing as can't," I argue as I continue to push her past her limits.

"Kam!" She squirms beneath me, but I don't let up. I know she can come again, and I'm just the man to make her.

A light sheen of sweat tickles my brow and my chest as my heart pounds to the same rhythm of my cock. Despite all her protests, Laney's body responds. Like it always does. She's moaning and writhing, digging her nails into my wrist as her pussy strangles me to death.

"Kam! Fuck! Fuck! Fuck!" She comes so damn hard she literally petrifies. Her arousal drenches my finger and my throbbing erection, and just when I can't hold back any longer, when I have restrained myself to the point I'm in pain, I let go. All the energy I possess pools in my lower abdomen and flushes out through my orgasm. My violent thrusts jerk Laney forward. Once, twice, three time's a charm. I come inside the woman I'm going to spend the rest of my life with. It's a mind-numbing mix, an emotional and physical clash of the titans. Every part of me hums and buzzes and vibrates as I'm demolished by the wrecking ball of my release.

I collapse on top of Laney, entirely shattered, the air thin and my body spent. Kissing my way lazily across her back, we lie sexually satisfied in silence.

"Mmm," Laney sighs, fatigued but content. Her skin so soft and smooth. I could skim my lips over it for hours. "You're going to have to carry me around everywhere tomorrow. I'm not going to be able to walk."

I smile against her. "I'll carry you anywhere."

She lifts her head and looks at me out of the corner of her eye. "I know you would."

"I wasn't sure you were going to say yes," I confess in the dim bedroom light.

Laney pauses before shimmying out from underneath me and wrapping herself around me.

"When does Kamdyn Ellis ever not get what he wants?" She nuzzles her nose into my chest, and the affection is poignant. As much as I enjoy indulging in her body, it's her love I revel in.

"I didn't know how you were going to react to the worldwide stage."

"Did you think I was going to say no?" She sounds genuinely surprised.

I shrug. My huge frame dwarfing her in my arms. "I looked at it like throwing a touchdown. There's confidence but never certainty."

"I'll admit being on the field with all the cameras and lights and people and players was a bit overwhelming, but as soon as I saw you, all my shock and awe and fear disappeared." She places her fingers on my chin. "It didn't matter who was around us, all I saw was you." She kisses my jaw, and I tighten my hold. Laney has been there for me every second of the last two years. Through every grueling game. Victorious wins and heartbreaking losses. Weeks away from her on the road. Sore muscles, pain in the ass teammates, and quarterback groupies.

I was determined to be a great leader when I was traded to New York. But it wasn't all celebrations and ticker tape parades when I walked into the locker room that first day. I was replacing a senior player. A player who was respected, and up until my trade, confident he owned his position. But that all changed when I showed up. It was a rocky first year. Tabloid headlines littered the Internet about a rival between Alabama's golden boy and the seasoned vet with several Super Bowl rings. Not all the headlines were false. We did go toe to toe. He didn't like me, and he made it clear, but I wasn't going to let him get into my head. At least not at practice or during a game. Home was a different story. The tension took a toll on me. I hated being at odds with a fellow teammate, and Laney let me unload whenever I needed to. She listened, she supported me, and she offered her advice. Which was pretty damn good. Being attached to a pro anything is a challenge in itself. Being the girlfriend—now fiancée—of the Kamdyn Ellis brand is a whole other universe. We are constantly in the public eye. Royalty of the American kind. We may not wear crowns, but we are revered. All because I can throw a pigskin farther and with more accuracy than any QB before me. I never asked to be a celebrity. I just wanted to play football. But I was born under a spotlight, and I'm meeting my fate head on.

My biggest blessing, though, is having a woman as strong and tenacious as Laney by my side. And there is no way in hell, under any circumstance, I'm going to let her go. I lost her once, never again. She'd have to tase me and bury me alive in order to leave. I hope it never comes to anything like that. But both our parents are divorced, so I understand what this next step means for the two of us. We talked briefly about getting married, and a core concern was commitment. And I don't mean commitment to each other. I mean commitment that when the going gets tough, we don't just get going. I've been successful in every other aspect of my life, and I want my marriage to be my greatest triumph.

"Go to sleep, Lemon." I press a firm kiss on her head.

"Are you actually going to let me stay asleep this time?"

"No promises." I grin.

Chapter THREE

LANEY

I AM A SURVIVOR of Kamdyn Ellis's core killing workout. Barely.

My lower body hasn't hurt this much since . . . I can't remember when. My very large, very affectionate, fiancé showed me just how much he loved me last night. Over and over again. Not that I'm complaining. I just wish crossing my legs didn't feel so uncomfortable, especially when I'm surrounded by mine and Kam's entire family.

Currently, I'm sitting at a large, round table with my father, Celebrity Chef Riley, and Kam's mother—who have been dating for the last few years—Kam's father, Steve, his wife Marcy, and Kam's younger brothers, Trevor and Luke.

It's a celebration brunch. For our engagement and Kam's win. It's not often we have our entire family in one place, so it's nice to take advantage of this time. Even if the entire restaurant is gawking at us. Kam is recognized wherever we go. It's hard to miss a six-foot-two quarterback with model good looks and charismatic personality. Especially when his face is plastered all over the tri-state area. He's as much of a hometown celebrity in New York as he was in Alabama. Even more so now that he's a pro.

The only person missing is my mom, who should be here any minute. She flew in from Hong Kong last night, so I imagine the jet lag is slowing her down.

The low hum of chatter in the bright, airy restaurant and the joyful energy at the table creates the perfect blend of momentary perfection. Kam is laughing and joking with his brothers. My father is sharing his newest culinary venture, while I sip on the most heavenly, blood-orange mimosa.

"Doing okay, Lemon? You're quiet," Kam drawls as he slides his hand up the inside of my thigh under the table. The light contact makes me flinch. My muscles are seriously sore. We both acknowledge my response. A secretive little smile skirts across Kam's lips.

"I'm fine." I suppress a smirk. "I'm just taking it all in."

"Having second thoughts about officially becoming an Ellis?"

"Of course not." I tap his stone bicep. "Laney Ellis has a great ring." I steal a sip of my cocktail.

"Yes, it does." Kam steals a kiss on my cheek. The whole table becomes quiet. Kam and I quickly turn our attention to the audience in front of us. Everyone is smiling.

"What?" Kam barks out a laugh, and the silence dissipates.

"We're just all so happy for you. For the two of you." My father raises his champagne glass. I try not to blush, but I fail miserably.

The maître d' appears in the middle of the attention onslaught, saving me from prolonged focus. The man, dressed in a tan suit, whispers something in Kam's ear. He looks toward the entrance and then smiles.

"Laney, your mom is here."

I whip my head in the same direction as Kam's gaze and see her walking through the restaurant. Tall and statuesque, dressed in an all-white jumper.

"Thank you, we're good." I hear Kam relay to the maître d' as I rise to my feet and stride excitedly in her direction. It's been six months since I've seen her, and for some reason, out of the blue, all I want to do is hug her.

"Hi, baby." She embraces me as I all but run into her arms.

"I'm glad you're here." I release her and look into the face that is so similar to mine. We have the same dark hair, blue eyes, and wide smile.

"There isn't any place I'd rather be." She holds onto my upper arms lightly. "I watched you on TV this morning. That was quite the proposal."

"Kam loves a spectacle." Our engagement was splashed all over the news more than the game. Only Kam could outshine a championship win.

"I sort of think he loves you, too." She scrunches her nose.

"Yeah, maybe a little." I laugh. "Let's go sit. We were waiting for you to order."

"Great, I'm starving and in desperate need of caffeine."

"You've come to the right place." I lead her by the hand to the table.

Kam stands and greets my mom with a bear hug and a kiss. Even though they've only met a handful of times, it's clear he's fond of her. Kam is hard not to like, and the same goes for my mom. She may be a pit bull when it comes to business, but she's a puppy dog when it comes to me. She says her pleasant hellos to everyone else at the table then takes a seat in the empty chair next to me.

"Okay, let's see it." She holds out her manicured hand. Everything about my mother's appearance screams refined and professional and put together.

I place my palm in hers, and she inspects the massive square diamond on my finger, blinding everyone in the room.

"Gorgeous."

"Riley and my mom helped me pick it out," Kam offers.

"Oh?" She smiles, but there's a hint of sadness in her eyes. Why? "You three make a good team."

"We have our moments." Kam's mom places her hand affectionately on my father's arm.

"Laney is very lucky to have you." Her expression displays happiness, but her eyes? There's an emotion she's hiding behind her eyes. I'm sure no one else notices but me. My mom has been physically absent from my life since before I started high school. She's a career woman, and her goals and aspirations were just as large and challenging as my father's. They both have monumental drive. That seems to be a theme with the people I love. Bigger than life. But in saying that, she's still my mom. I know her. I can read her the same way she can read me.

She's always been there for me. No matter the time or what side of the world she was on, she always made me a priority. There were countless three a.m. phone calls, video chats over a gallon of ice cream, and vacations to the most beautiful parts of the world. Our relationship is unconventional, but so are the relationships I have with my father and my fiancé. Just because they aren't cookie cutter doesn't mean they are any less important. And I manage each of those just fine. I'm pretty independent, and my career is just as important to me as my mom's is to her. Kam's is to him. And my father's is to him. I may not live in the spotlight, or travel all over creation, but I love what I do. Being an architect is my dream, and I'm living it the same way everyone else around me is.

The waiter appears to take my mother's drink order. Once she's settled, the conversation niceties begin.

We spend the morning catching up over decadent French toast, pancakes stacked a mile high, and fruit so fresh it tastes like it was just picked from the vine. Kam eats enough for three people. He's changed so much over the last two years. He's always been tall and athletic, but this new level of training has transformed him dramatically. His arms and chest are almost double the size, and his waist is leaner, more tapered than it was before. He is all male, all athlete, all super-star.

And all mine.

I admire the diamond sparkling like fire on my finger. It's beautiful yes, and I love it, but I love the person who gave it to me more.

"Have you two thought about a date yet?" My mother's question cuts through my daydreaming.

"Um, no." I glance at Kam. "We have one big event to get through first before we start planning another one." I can't even imagine what the next few weeks are going to be like. Kam prepping for the championship game was intense enough. Preparing for the Super Bowl? I don't even want to think about it until tomorrow. I have a feeling I'm going to be a football widow until the clock times out.

"Well, not to overstep or be that pushy mother"—she rolls her eyes and does this little gesture with her head—"but I took the liberty of calling a friend of mine. She's one of the most sought-after wedding planners in New York." She adds quickly. "Anyway, she told me she has an opening June 6th. So, I booked her."

"June 6th of what year?" my father asks as I stare at my mom.

"This year. I know it's soon—"

"It's less than six months from now," I point out.

"I know. And you don't have to commit to anything. But she sent me this picture of the Conservatory Gardens in Central Park." She pulls out her phone and brings up a picture. "It just looks stunning." She shows the aerial view of the extravagant gardens. They're bursting with rows of white and purple flowery trees, French-style gardens, and the greenest grass you have ever laid eyes on.

"Wow!" Kam takes her phone and inspects the image further. "This would be an awesome place for the wedding."

"And June would be the perfect time," my mom hints.

"I agree, June is perfect. But . . . this June?" I weigh the option. "There's so much planning. I have a huge proposal coming up at work. And Kam? The Super Bowl?"

"Sweetie." My mother takes my hand. "I do not want you to do anything that makes you uncomfortable. I just thought I would help lessen the load reaching out to a pro who is accustomed to working with celebrities." She nods at Kam. "She would do most of the grunt work. You just have to pick out the details."

"That does sound less stressful," Kam considers, handing my mother back her phone.

I'm at a loss for words for a moment. "This June wouldn't be too soon for you?" I ask Kam in all seriousness.

His baby blues burn with affection in the sunlight. "Lemon, I would go to city hall tomorrow if that's what you wanted. I don't care when it happens, or where it happens, just as long as it happens."

The table goes quiet for the second time this morning. My cheeks are going to blister from embarrassment if I'm kept under all this scrutiny.

"Okay. June 6th, it is," I cave, my heart pounding a mile a minute.

"Excuse me." An unfamiliar voice pulls my attention away from Kam. A young boy, no more than ten, is standing behind us, bouncing back and forth nervously with a pen and paper in his hand. "I'm sorry to bother you." His words are shaky, not nervous but upset.

"It's okay, bud." Kam turns and smiles. "Would you like an autograph?"

"Yes, please." The boy's brown eyes water. "My dad was a huge fan. We watched your first game at Alabama and haven't missed one since."

"Well, that's awesome." Kam takes the pen and paper. "What's your name?"

"Tommy. Tommy Miller."

"Well, Tommy Miller"—Kam scribbles his name on the small white paper—"where's your dad? I'd like to meet him, too."

A tear drops from the child's eyes. "He's not here. He went to heaven a few months ago."

Kam pauses. We all do. "I'm very sorry to hear that." Kam clears his throat.

"I'm one of your biggest fans. I'm gonna watch all your games. For my dad."

Kam turns his entire body toward the brown-haired boy.

"I appreciate that. I'm gonna play my heart out for you. And your dad." Then Kam does something that breaks my heart. He hugs him. Engulfs him in his arms and gives him a fierce squeeze. Kam can't see it, but I can. I can see the brief solace on the boy's face as his hero connects with him on a human level.

This, ladies and gentlemen, is exactly the reason why I have zero doubts about becoming Mrs. Kamdyn Ellis.

Chapter FOUR

LANEY

THE DAY'S FESTIVITIES AREN'T through yet.

After an eventful brunch, Kam and I had about five minutes of downtime before we had to shower and change for a celebration gala the team is hosting in New York City.

I will be the first to admit my fiancé cleans up well. At heart, Kam is a down-home southern boy. He loves his broken-in denim jeans and casual T-shirts. But he has no issue adapting to the part of dapper gentleman draped in an Armani suit. He wears many hats, and owns each and every one of them the same way he owns the football field.

Currently, Kam is owning the room. He's the man of the hour. Sophomore year in the NFL and he's leading his team to the big game. The excitement is palpable. Throw our high-profile engagement in the mix, and it's a full-on electric storm. For me, anyway. Social media has been buzzing since last night. Every media outlet has played and replayed the proposal repeatedly. While driving through Times Square, the ticker congratulated the team on their win and Kam on our engagement as the

Jumbotron simultaneously broadcasted a bigger-than-life still of Kam on one knee and me a delightful shade of red.

My life is surreal sometimes.

Like right now, for instance. I'm surrounded by models and actresses and reality stars fawning over my hand and the diamond you can probably see from Mars. All the wives and girlfriends of the players who have become part of my extended family.

"It is gorgeous." Chris, a six-foot-tall, statuesque model gushes. The brunette with the most beautiful, buttery-olive skin you've ever laid eyes on nearly yanks my arm off.

The rock on her finger is just as impressive. She's engaged to Martell Lewis, or Telly as we all know him, one of the top ten running backs in the league. I know most of the players' significant others. We've been thrown together in a mishmash of public events and dinner parties the last two years. "And I can't believe you have a date set already! You and Kam have been engaged for twenty-four hours!" Mia chimes in. She's a reality star who won that around-the-world challenge. She met her husband, Robert, the team's center, when he guest-starred on the show. Apparently, it was history after that. They eloped six weeks after she won and have been going strong ever since.

"That wasn't planned. My mom pulled a string, and Kam hopped on board." I reach for my drink on the bar. The girls have been crowding me since the moment I walked into the room.

"At least football season will be over." Chris huffs, sipping on her champagne.

"Hey, you were the one who wanted to get married on a leap year," I remind her.

"I know, but who knew they were going to go to the freaking Super Bowl. The tone of my wedding seriously depends on the outcome of that game."

"It will be fine." Mia waves her off. "No matter what, everyone will be blitzed. It will either be from joyous celebration or drowning their sorrows. Drunk at a wedding sounds like a win-win to me."

"Dear Lord, please let it be from joyous celebration," Chris prays.

"If I know Kam, it will be. Nothing is going to stop him from getting that win. He's like a bull seeing red."

"Awww, and then you guys will have the perfect happily ever after," Mia pokes fun. "The Super Bowl MVP and his bride."

"You are lucky I love you, 'cause I sorta want to throw my drink in your face." I laugh.

"Save it for later. The managers will totally have a cow if there's a bitch fight at the bar." We all giggle in great spirits. "Could you imagine?"

"I can see the headlines now." Chris snorts. "Girls' fight night at celebration gala. Which NFL hottie hits the hardest?"

"Definitely me," I claim the title.

"Laugh it up now, ladies." Monique, an ex-lingerie model and wife of the quarterback Kam replaced, tosses in her two cents. She hasn't said much all night. Usually she's a social butterfly, but she's just been hovering by the bar, sipping her martini, a long, silk champagne gown draped over her lean body. "Everything is all wonderful in the beginning." Her French accent drips with disdain. "You have kids, a beautiful home, the American dream, so you say. Then you find out it's all a ruse. A scam, because your wonderful husband has been cheating on you the whole time. You are the fool, and everyone knew it but you." She drains the vodka from her glass. "Demand a pre-nup." She bumps into Mia then me before she struts off, clearly pissed and clearly drunk. We all stare at her bare back as she walks right past her husband without a second glance and out of the lavish ballroom.

A dampening silence blankets our little group. Even though none of us will admit it, what Monique said is true. Being a professional athlete and being faithful is a rare occurrence. We've all heard stories or seen it firsthand. I look over at Kam laughing and talking, living in the moment. His stock just went up twenty thousand points. Women throw themselves at him on a daily basis despite our very public relationship. Groupies don't care if you're married, engaged, or have a girlfriend, and a lot of times, neither do the players. My only comfort is knowing cheating isn't Kam's style. It never has been, but it doesn't mean temptation isn't ever present. It's front and center in this world. And I'm not naïve enough to pretend it doesn't exist. Or that he isn't confronted. I just have to trust in him. Trust in us, and hope we don't end up like my parents. Or his.

KAM

I SIT AT THE kitchen counter watching the sun rise over the Hudson River. I have an early flight to Tennessee to prepare for this weekend's game. I've been putting in overtime at the gym and with my offensive coach to hone my concentration and stay in the zone. Miami is going to be a tough team to beat, but there are chinks in their armor that can work to my advantage. I just have to know when and how to use it against them during the game. Football is so much more than just brute strength and speed. For a quarterback, it's a symphony of passes, fast footwork, lightning-quick hands, and split-second response times.

I plan to be on-point 'cause nothing is going to take this victory away from me.

My attention settles on the signed Dan Marino football sitting proudly on the bookshelf next to the TV. It's one of my prized possessions. Second to Laney, of course. He signed it at a benefit, and then auctioned it off for charity. I made sure I was the highest bidder. He joked afterwards that he would have signed a football for me for free.

But I didn't mind paying. Just being in the presence of one of my heroes was enough. Ironically, Miami is who we're facing in the big game.

My life can be pretty perfect at times. Like right now. I have my health, my girl, and the career I've always wanted.

I reflect on all that I've been blessed with in the quiet moments that are short lived. I hear Laney's heels against the hardwood floor before she appears in the kitchen. I'm already smiling.

"Morning," she chirps as she heads straight for the coffee maker.

"Morning," I respond, drinking in her lean form. She's dressed in a white, button-up shirt with ruffles down the front, a skin-tight pencil skirt, and black high heels. She's professionally hot in my opinion. And let's be honest, my opinion is the only one that counts.

"Whatcha doin' here all alone?" Laney sidles up beside me with her coffee cup.

"Nuthin', just taking in the peace and quiet for a minute." I slip my arm around her waist and suction cup a kiss to her neck.

She giggles lightly, squirming in my arm.

"Quit that. You're gonna give me a hickey."

"And what's wrong with that? I'm leaving in a few hours. I need to mark what's mine."

"You have marked what's yours. You proposed to me in front of half the free world. I'm locked down and everyone knows it." She blows on her steaming coffee. The warm, fragrant smell wafting around us.

That statement makes the caveman in me bang his chest. Laney is mine. She always has been, and she always will be.

"Leaving is the worst part of my job."

"Every job has a downside. Even when you're a pro football player." I get very little sympathy from her. "You'll only be gone a few days. I fly out on Friday," she reminds me as she sips on her coffee. Her big blue eyes holding mine over the rim of the cup. "I'm sort of looking forward to getting away."

"If you're looking for some R and R, I don't think you're going to find it in Nashville," I break the news. "It's going to be insanity."

"I'm not looking for R and R; I'm looking to escape." She chuckles.

"From? Is work stressing you out?"

"Work . . . and my mom," she mumbles. "I never thought I'd say this, but she's driving me crazy. Ever since brunch, she has been texting and emailing me nonstop with wedding stuff. Dresses, flowers, cakes." Laney's pretty eyes grow wide. "She's momzilla of the bride."

I can't help but laugh. "She's just excited."

"I know. But it's just so unlike her to be so . . . involved." She bites her lip. "That sounds terrible. But I'm not sure how to feel about this new helicopter side of her."

I, unfortunately, don't have much advice to give on this front. "The only thing I can say is it's a good thing we're getting married sooner than later." I go in for another bite on her neck.

"Kam!" Laney squeals. "You're going to make me spill coffee all over myself!"

"That was my evil plan all along. Get you naked before I leave."

"Not happening, All-star." She pushes me away playfully. "I have to get to work, and you have a plane to catch."

"There are other flights." I draw her closer to me.

"Lucky for you. Unlucky for me there aren't other jobs. I have a ton of work to do before I leave. I really want to impress the bosses on this downtown project. I have this redesign I want to pitch, and I'm so nervous. It's a little out of the box for a conservative building."

I actually understood that sentence. Usually when Laney talks about work, I'm thrown off a little. Architecture and design are incredibly detailed and technical concentrations. And although I'm not a complete dumb jock, Laney and her career can make me feel like that sometimes. I get her drive, and that's a common enough language for me.

"Lemon, I have no doubt you are going to wow them. I've seen your designs. They're incredible. You have nothing to worry about."

"Kam." She drops her head to mine. "Sometimes I wish I could bottle your optimism and confidence."

"It's a southern thing, sugar." I kiss her cheek.

"Don't call me sugar."

I roll my eyes. "When are you going to get over that?"

"Never."

"Yankee pessimist. That's your problem," I accuse.

"Definitely. It's who I am. It's also why I have you. To inject some laid-back southern style into me."

"Lemon. Is this verbal foreplay? 'Cause you know I will never deny injecting you with some laid-back southern style. It might be a little rough at first, but you'll be as lazy as a house cat by the time I'm done with you." I stand and grab her.

"Kam." She places one small hand on my massive chest. "I wasn't insinuating anything." A piece of dark hair falls over her eye. She blows it away as she tries to fend me off. But all that talk of injecting has got me going.

"I'm not going to see you for five days, Lemon."

"You'll live." She places her coffee down carefully while trying to escape from my hold. Multitasker, my Lemon.

"I'm not sure I will." I crush her against my body and attack her mouth, licking up the coffee taste and savoring the softness of her lips.

Laney's defenses drop as my persistence wears her down. "Right here, right now, real quick." I turn her around and bend her over the granite island.

"Kam," she scolds, but doesn't stop me from lifting her skirt and sliding my fingers into her panties. I rub the sweet spot between her legs until she's moaning and wet and pushing against my hand. She has no idea what she does to me sometimes. Giving me what I want, whenever I want.

"Fuck, Kam." Laney shivers, her muscles tightening around my jabbing fingers.

"It's going to be so worth being late," I hiss into her ear as I shove the satin and lace material down her thighs.

"Fast, Kam." She huffs.

"Don't tell me what to do, sugar. I'm enjoying the view." Laney naked from the waist down, her muscular calves carved out from the height of the high black heels. My cock pulses with a rush of blood. "You know how to drive a man nuts without even trying." I slide my sweatpants down and palm my erection.

"Some girls just got it like that." She grins at me over her shoulder, her bright blue eyes heavy with lust.

"You had me from the moment I met you." I slip urgently inside her. "And every fucking second after that." I drive into her forcefully, over and over, Laney's body jerking with every thrust. We fuck hard and fast, her arousal drenching me from base to tip.

"It's always so fucking good with you." I anchor my hand on her throat and pound away until she comes. It doesn't take long.

"Kam, fuck! Kamdyn, fuck!" When she screams my whole name, she explodes, shattering me right along with her. We climax together, a mixture of grunts and groans and sighs and moans filling the room.

Laney collapses forward on the cool granite as she catches her breath. Her body limp but every bit still as enticing. I'm reluctant to pull out, so instead I swim in the sea of our aftermath, sliding in and out of her pussy as easily as a warm spoon through honey.

"Now I can leave in good conscious."

"Why is that?" Laney asks with her cheek still plastered to the countertop.

"Because my woman is sated and satisfied." I lean over and press my chest to her back.

"And late. Don't forget late."

"Just for work." I wink.

"Definitely just for work," she adamantly agrees. "And definitely sated and satisfied." Laney closes her eyes and sighs. I swell with pride. That look on Laney's face is as thrilling as throwing a touchdown pass.

"Think about me while I'm gone?" I kiss her cheek, her jaw, and her neck.

"Like I'll be able to think about anything else." She smiles blissfully.

THE LAST FIVE DAYS have been nothing but running drills, conditioning drills, and throwing sessions. Sixty-minute throw ins—deep, shallow, and combo—piled on top of agility training, followed by years and years of films.

I am wiped, but oh-so-fucking wired.

It's midnight, and I'm supposed to be sleeping, but all I can think about is a game-winning touchdown and celebrating with Laney on my arm.

She was supposed to fly in this morning, but she got caught up at work and had to delay. Of all the days. I know her big project is important to her, and I want to be supportive, but I also want to be selfish and have her here with me.

Tomorrow. She's hopping on a six a.m. flight, so she should be here by noon. Twelve hours. I have lasted five days without her, I can last twelve more hours. Hopefully. I grab my cock; he misses the hell out of her, too.

I roll over onto my side and hug one of the extra pillows, attempting to fall asleep once again. My body is exhausted, but my mind is stuck in overdrive.

After a few frustrating minutes of rocking and counting push-ups in my head, I finally begin to drift off.

I sink into the mattress as my muscles relax, and just as I submerge into sleep, a click startles me awake. My eyelids fly open, but I don't move an inch. I've heard rumors of player pranks over the last few days. The guys blowing off steam after a grueling workout or practice.

Practical jokers they think they are. Our team is young and ambitious and sometimes needs to be herded like cats. But when we play as a collective whole, we are nearly unstoppable. We've formed a special kind of bond that's not easily achieved on any level, but our personalities mesh exceptionally well, and we all have the same goal. Win. That's the endgame. Not fame or ego or popularity. That all comes with winning. It was one of the first things I told my team, and the statement surprisingly resonated. I'm ready to lead them. I'm ready to win.

I hear footsteps coming closer to the bed. They think they're going to catch my off guard. Little do they know, they have another thing coming.

Just as the body hovers over me, I strike my hand out like a snake and grab behind their thigh. There's a shriek, then a thud, then an, "Ouch, shit."

I shoot out of bed. "Lemon?"

"Yeah?" Laney grumbles.

"What the hell were you doing?" I toss the covers, switch on the bed lamp, and reach for her.

"I was going to sneak into bed and surprise you. So much for that." She rubs her ass. She hit the ground hard.

"I'm so sorry, baby." I pull her up off the floor and into my arms. "I thought you were one of the guys fucking with me. They've been pulling pranks all week."

"Well, remind me to thank them very much for my black and blue butt," she whines adorably.

"You weren't supposed to get in until tomorrow."

"Surprise," she drawls dryly. "I caught a red-eye. I missed you. And I wanted to be here for you. I figured you'd be out cold from all the training and practice. I wanted to be snuggled up against you when you woke up."

"Good plan. Bad execution." I laugh.

"Obviously." She frowns, still rubbing her bum.

"Let me take care of that for you." I take over rubbing her ass. Laney's wearing a casual T-shirt and skin-tight yoga pants. I can feel the heat of her skin right through the stretchy material.

"I've been tossing and turning all night," I share my snoozing dilemma.

"You've been having trouble sleeping?" She touches my face tenderly.

"Just tonight. I think all the pressure is finally catching up to me."

"Only two nights before the biggest game of your life? Pansy," she teases. Jesus, I missed her.

"I'm human." I pin her to the mattress, biting her neck until she's giggling and squirming.

"I forget sometimes."

"Don't be smart." I bite then suck her skin, and she squeals.

"You're going to give me a hickey!"

"Like in high school," I reminisce.

"Those were never visible."

"Mmmm, I know." I roll on top of her and press my pulsing cock between her legs.

"Someone missed me." Laney slides her arms around my neck and flexes her hips. The pressure is skull-splitting.

"Fuck yes, I did." The groan that escapes my throat is volcanic.

"Maybe I can help you with your little insomnia problem?"

"What do you have in mind?" As if I couldn't guess.

Laney urges me off her. The dim light from the lamp allowing me to see the lust and desire for control in her bright blue eyes.

"Lie back." Laney pushes on my chest, and my senses oscillate from her command.

Fuck, she has no idea how much I need this. How much I need her.

Laney kisses her way slowly down my bare chest, running the tip of her tongue seductively over the ridges of my abs, then teases the exposed skin right above the elastic of my boxer briefs.

A slow death. That's what she has planned for me.

There are worse ways to go.

When Laney peels my underwear away I become a slave under her hand. I'll do anything she asks, execute anything she demands. This woman owns me, and I don't give a flying fuck who knows it.

"Lemon." I huff as she wraps both hands around my cock and licks the tip of its engorged head.

"Mmm?" she responds, her mouth a little busy. I stretch out in total bliss as she strokes and tongues and jerks my erection.

"Jesus, baby." She sucks me off until I'm about ready to explode, my cock throbbing, my fingers and toes curling. And just when I feel the first tingles of my orgasm, Laney stops. "Fucker." I grab my shaft in pain.

Above me, Laney strips off her clothes. Her shirt, her bra, her pants, and her underwear all disappear within a matter of seconds.

"I was going to make you come, but I want you inside me." Her voice is breathy and full of want.

"I would never say no to that." I massage both her bare breasts as she straddles me. This woman and her fucking unbelievable body. It's complete euphoria as her soft, wet heat engulfs my cock, and when I'm completely buried inside her, we both expel a tortured moan.

It's stimulation overload as Laney begins to ride me. My muscles coiling like a metal spring from the pressure of my arousal.

I sit up, wrapping my arms around Laney's waist just to get closer, deeper, demand more of her.

"Kam." She grips my hair and whimpers as her clit rubs against my pelvis and her body rocks against mine. She's as close as I am.

"I'm right here." I grip her tighter, a statue made purely of pleasure. Her pussy clenches around my cock, and the tightness forces me to groan. "Let go, Laney. Let fucking go." I clench my jaw as the warm, wet call of her body pulls the pin on my control.

Laney comes as hard as I do, so loud and explosive I'm confident she woke the neighbors. But who cares? They should be so lucky. Or at least envious.

I collapse onto the pillow, taking Laney's limp form with me. We're sweaty and out of breath, but both supremely satisfied.

She's just what I needed.

She's always what I need.

I yawn, and Laney smiles. "Mission accomplished. Operation Sleep underway." She giggles.

I snicker as I tangle my fingers in her long, dark hair. "I suppose you're going to take credit for my Super Bowl win as well?"

"Of course. Behind every great man is an even greater woman," she murmurs smugly. I think my super ego is rubbing off on her. But I can't argue, Laney is definitely a huge part of my success and a key ingredient in the formula. "Now go to sleep, All-star. You need your rest. You have a Super Bowl championship to win."

"No pressure," I exhale.

"None."

LANEY

THIS GAME HAS BEEN brutal to watch.

I don't think anyone expected it to be such a grudge match. Including Kam.

He's playing his heart out and taking a beating while doing it. My anxiety has spiked through the roof. Last down, he was sacked after he threw the ball with no flag on the play. These refs suck. Dirty as it was, what really scared me is that he took longer than usual to get up. I bit all the gel polish off my nails in the third quarter and then started right in on my real nails in the fourth.

It's tied, and there's a minute left on the clock. It's like swallowing pins and needles. I don't know how Kam deals with the pressure.

My father rubs my shoulders as we watch from the skybox. My mother is on my left and Kam's mom is on my right.

"He's gonna pull it out. If anyone can do it, Kam can," my father reassures me. His southern drawl soothing as always. I know he's right. On a football field, Kam is Superman.

We are all aware how much he wants this win. I know how hard he's worked and the pedestal he's been put on by his fans.

I find myself praying as the ball is snapped. I stop breathing as I watch Kam quickly dance left then right, a barrage of players moving around him and heading toward him. He launches it into the end zone, directly at Wiley who is wide open. Everyone tenses. It looks good. Really, really, good . . . time stands still . . . it's . . . it's . . . intercepted!

All my muscles sag as I watch the running back from Miami burn grass down the field for a sixty-yard touchdown.

Tears burn my eyes as the clock runs out. Kam drops to his knees clutching his facemask on the sixty-yard line while Miami celebrates its victory. You can hear a pin drop in the box. I press my palms to the glass as I look down at Kam, helplessly.

I don't think devastated even begins to describe what I'm feeling. And I know whatever disappointment I'm feeling, Kam is experiencing it a thousand times worse.

And there's nothing I can do. There's nothing any of us can do.

THE LAST THREE WEEKS have been . . . challenging.

Kam hasn't taken his championship loss very well. Neither has the media. Not even an hour after the game, headlines like "Kam the Scam" and "Alabama Golden Boy Not So Golden" were popping up everywhere. It's amazing how easily news outlets can turn on you when not even twenty-four hours before they were singing your praises.

I confiscated all the electronics in the house and hid all the remotes so Kam wouldn't torture himself with the scrutiny. He's tortured enough. He's his biggest critic, and he is coming down on himself hard.

He's barely left the house, eaten, slept, or showered. I try to be understanding and supportive. I know he'll come through, it will just take some time. How much? Hopefully not too-too much. It's already been three weeks. Kam usually bounces back from adversity quickly and stronger than before. But this—this is killing him.

I miss my high-spirited, optimistic egomaniac. Not that I would tell him that. I know he has to grieve. A dream died, and that's as real as losing a loved one.

I watch quietly for a few seconds in the doorway of our bedroom as Kam mindlessly packs a weekender bag. Something that used to take him minutes has taken nearly an hour. He's lost in thought. Lost in self-deprecation. He sits down on the edge of our bed flipping a balled-up pair of white socks the same way he would handle a football. My heart breaks. I hate seeing him like this. He's so much better than all of this and everyone knows it. He'll realize it, too. I'm sure of it.

I saunter over to where he's sitting and slip myself between his legs. He looks up at me forlornly. It's so unlike the man I love. Touching his stubbly cheek, I deliver him a warm, tender smile. I'm rewarded with one in return. It isn't as brilliant as it usually is, but we're making progress.

"I don't want to go," Kam confesses.

"You need to go," I urge. "You need to blow off some steam and decompress. Go be with your guys. Drink, laugh, have fun. It's a bachelor party. Show Telly a good time." I clutch his face. "And have one yourself."

Kam exhales. He's mustering his drive.

"I'm going to miss you." He rests his hands on my hips.

I lean over and whisper seductively in his ear, "It's only two days, and when you get home, we'll have a good time of our own."

Kam emits a little growl as he digs his fingertips into my waist. I smile to myself, my All-star is coming around.

We share an elongated, steamy kiss that fogs the bedroom windows and leaves me winded.

"Are you sure you want to wait until I get back?" Kam asks with his eyes closed and breathing labored. I can't help but respond, and just as I go to climb on top of him, our intercom buzzes.

"Shit. That's Rodney." Kam falls back onto our shiny, sparkly comforter I insisted on having.

"Better get that." I pat his chest.

"Yeah," he huffs, disappointed.

"Oh, stop," I scold him. "Go. Please have some fun. Crush it on the golf course. It will feed your competitive appetite."

"I guess." He sits up and steals one more emotive kiss before the buzzer goes off again. "Fucker."

I laugh before running to get the door. Our condo isn't huge, but it's definitely spacious enough with its large, modern, eat-in kitchen, living room with views of the Hudson River, and double-port entryway. I swing open the front door to a smiling Rodney. Rodney Pines is a running back for New York but a big ol' country boy at heart. He and Kam hit it off right away.

"Hey, Lanes! Is the man ready?" Rodney strolls in wearing a tight black T-shirt and worn out Levis.

"As I'll ever be." Kam appears in a very similar outfit, but his jeans are cut a bit more modern and hang lower on his hips. The man wears clothes like a damn model, but it's the fitted baseball cap that gets me. He's adorably hot when he's not even trying.

"What are you grinning at?" Kam asks as he drops his bag at my feet.

"My Mister Perfect." I dot a kiss on his lips.

"You know I'm not perfect." His tone is distressed.

"You know that's not true," I disagree. "You're perfect for me."

"Awww, you two are so nauseatingly cute. Let me take a picture." Rodney pretends to snap away.

"You and your pictures." Kam swipes at him.

"Everyone needs a hobby." Rodney picks up Kam's bag. "I also think I threw up in my mouth a little."

"Don't be jealous, Rodney," I tease him.

"Trust me, I'm not." He's somewhat serious. "We're gonna be late. I don't want to hear a plane full of complaints."

"I'm with ya." Kam slides an arm around my waist. "What are ya gonna do while I'm away?" He kisses my neck.

"Think naughty thoughts about you," I announce just to make Rodney uncomfortable.

"Aww, jeez. Maybe I'm a little jealous now." Rodney slings Kam's bag over his shoulder.

"I'll meet you at the car." Kam chases Rodney away.

"You got five minutes."

"Plenty of time." Kam presses me against the wall, a wicked look in his light blue eyes.

"Not nearly enough time," I dispute.

"Seriously, dry heaving here," Rodney yells from out of sight.

Kam and I both crack up. It's good to see him smile. Genuinely smile.

"Lemon, don't send me away knowing you're going to be all hot and bothered."

"Don't worry about me. I can take care of myself."

"That's what I'm afraid of. Taking care of you is my job."

"And you do it exceptionally well." I lean in and press my lips to his, slipping just the tip of my tongue into his mouth.

"Don't tease me, Laney."

"I'm not. I'm sending you away with expectations."

"Very dirty expectations."

"As dirty as you want them to be," I promise.

"Jesus, I love you, woman."

"I'm one of a kind," I toy.

"That is the fucking truth." He crushes me against the wall with another heart-stopping embrace. "Are you sure five minutes isn't enough time?" Kam presses his raging erection against me.

"Definitely not. I don't want Rodney pulling you off me right in the middle."

"A fucking herd of wild horses couldn't pull me away while I'm inside you."

Kam's phone rings. And there is reality returning.

"Go," I encourage him. "Sunday night I'm all yours."

"You're all mine for the rest of your life." He steps back, adjusts himself, then takes my hand and kisses my engagement ring.

"I've been all yours since the moment we met," I reluctantly admit.

"Don't I know it." Kam grins triumphantly. Such a cocky shit. But that's why I love him. His confidence shines like the sun, and his heart is as big and as deep as the ocean. He's one of a kind.

Kam pulls his phone out of his back pocket. "I'm comin'."

He hangs up then groans. It's sexy, even though it's a frustrated sound.

"I'm going to start a wedding registry with my mom later today," I reveal my real plans. "I'll pick out a few things, and then we can pick out the rest together."

"Sounds like a plan. Your mom will like that. Quality time."

"Yeah. She's all about this wedding. It's pretty nice having her around."

"I can tell how much you like spending time with her." Kam swipes the pad of his thumb across my bottom lip.

"I am overly blessed with amazing people in my life."

"Lemon, it's us who're blessed. Trust me on that." Kam swipes his lips over mine this time. The sweet, loving contact makes my scalp tingle. "Make sure you put a sterling silver grill set on that registry. I'm planning on some big family cookouts in the future."

"I'm glad to hear that. I'll make sure to register for a 'Kiss the Cook' apron, too."

"Long as it's pink," Kam cracks.

"Done." I giggle. I plan to find one with ruffles, too. That image would go viral, no doubt.

Kam's phone rings again, and we both acknowledge it's really time for Kam to go.

"Be good. Miss me a lot." Kam steals one more kiss.

"You know I always do."

"Me, too, baby. Me, too."

Chapter SEVEN

KAM

I CLIMB THE STAIRS of the private jet right behind Rodney. We're the last to arrive, and as soon as we step inside the luxury liner, we're showered with boos and pelted with balled-up napkins.

"It was his fault!" Rodney throws me under the bus as he shields himself from the spray of white paper bullets. "He was all huggin' and kissin' on his girl." He wraps his arms around himself and makes kissy faces. I shove him.

"He's just complaining 'cause he's jealous."

"Just my dick is jealous. You have one fine piece of ass."

"Don't make me punch you for calling Laney a piece of ass."

"You won't have to, Q, she'll punch him herself!" Stone, one of the lineman, contributes to the conversation from the back of the plane.

"This is true," I agree with him. My girl is as rough and tumble as she is smart and feminine.

The whole team is stuffed into the rented plane for Telly's bachelor party. His wedding is next Saturday, so we are celebrating his last weekend of freedom. The alcohol is already flowing, the music is pumping, and there is a party vibe infecting the small space. Usually, I would jump right on the band wagon, but even though there is a smile on my face, my heart just isn't in it. Because all I see when I look at my fellow teammates' faces is failure. I failed them. I failed myself, and I failed New York's fans. Letting that win slip through my fingers tortures me every second of the day. I hear it, I see it, I feel it no matter where I am. Watching the ball sail into the hands of the opposing team's defender, an action which essentially relinquished the winning touchdown, will haunt me for the rest of my fucking life.

The rest of my fucking life.

Rodney and I sit in the last two open seats. They're white leather and sleek as hell. Telly didn't spare one expense. He went all out with the private charter, five-star hotel in Myrtle Beach, and a round of golf at the most high-end course in the area. We are going to be smokin' Cubans and sippin' Cognac all weekend long.

I want to embrace what Laney said, to have a good time. And I want to be in good spirits for Telly, too, but the black cloud of disappointment and defeat is pouring down on me constantly. I barely have enough air to breathe, but I keep pushing forward, hoping the storm will break. But blue skies aren't anywhere in sight.

"Drink, Q?" Robert, my center, asks with a head nod. "We got beer, beer, and more beer for the plane ride."

"Hmmm . . ." I contemplate. "I think I'll have a beer."

Rob launches a can at me. "Hey, keep up that show and you'll be QB next year." I crack it open, and it squirts a bit.

"Shit, please." He snorts. "Ain't no one can walk in the great Kamdyn Ellis's shoes."

Great. Yeah, right.

I don't entertain a response. I just smirk and sip my beer. It's ice cold and goes down way too fucking easy.

I feel Rodney scrutinize me, but I ignore him, pretending to enjoy myself like everyone else around me.

DINNER LAST NIGHT WAS delicious, and the Bloody Mary's on the course this morning are even better.

It's a beautiful, bright day. The sun is shining, the clouds are white and puffy, and the climate is perfectly comfortable.

I haven't had a chance to play golf in months, so I'm looking forward to swinging the clubs.

I tee up on the first hole and whack a beauty seventy-five yards. It drops right next to the green.

"Nice shot, QB." Telly clasps me on the shoulder.

"Thanks. Maybe if my football career doesn't work out, I have a future in golf."

"Man, you got jokes." Telly places his ball on the tee. He is wearing the loudest checkered pants known to man and the ugliest lime green shirt on the planet. Why golfing attire is so horrendous, I will never understand. And why men embrace it is an even bigger mystery.

"Yeah, jokes." Rodney gives me the same look now as he did on the plane. When I pointedly ignored him.

Our foursome consists of Rodney, Telly, myself, and Landon Knobs, a rookie from the Midwest who apparently has zero golfing experience. He can run like hell down a football field, though.

"Everyone take a step back," Rodney announces as Landon tees up.

"Shut up, dude. I got this."

"Mmm-hmm," Rodney vibrates. "I saw you at the driving range this morning. It was ugly."

"Fuck off." Landon swings, and the ball soars into the trees.

"That wasn't even in the general direction of the green!" Rodney explodes.

Landon turns around with a red face.

"Cut me some fucking slack. I've never done this before!"

"Obviously. That was just insulting. Bagger Vance is rolling over in his grave right now!"

Me and Telly can't help but snicker from the cart. This round is going to be comical if Rodney keeps riding Landon like this.

Three holes later, Landon is about ready to strangle Rodney. Or beat him to death with a club. He hasn't let up on him for a second, and the tension is running high.

"These two be acting a fool." Telly shakes his head as Rodney tries to direct Landon while he putts.

"I couldn't have said it better myself." I laugh as I remove my sunglasses to clean them. Just then I hear "Fore!" and before I know it, I'm choking and sputtering for air on the ground.

"Jesus Christ! You only call 'fore!' when you drive!" Rodney roars as the three of them hover over me. "You're a menace to society holding a fucking golf club."

I clutch my neck as the throbbing pain blinds me.

"Here." Telly comes and goes in a flash before pressing a handful of ice to the side of my neck. He must have grabbed it from the cooler on the cart. "Can you breathe, Q?"

I suck in a few deep breaths as my vision clears. "I'm good. Get me up."

Telly and Rodney haul me off the grass as I press the melting ice to my jugular.

"Q, I'm sorry. I didn't mean to . . . Rodney just pissed me off, and I fucking swung."

I hold my hand up. There feels like a lump forming in my throat. "It's okay," I assure Landon. "Karma, I'm sure."

All three of them look at me oddly.

"Did the ball hit your throat or your head?" Rodney asks.

"Throat. For sure." I drop my hand, and they all grimace.

"Shit, that looks like the most painful hickey on Earth."

"Crap." I pull my phone out and switch the camera view. Jesus. My neck is an angry black and blue, and if you look close enough, you can even see indentations from the divots on the golf ball.

"Keep some ice on it, Q. You,"—Rodney points to Landon—"I'm confiscating your clubs. You're a cerebral hemorrhage waiting to happen."

I wince, unpleasant memories from high school flooding me. I actually suffered from a cerebral hemorrhage and almost didn't live to tell about it.

"That's bullshit. If you would just lay off and let me play . . ." Landon rushes him, and Telly gets between them.

"Yo, chill. This is supposed to be fun. It's my bachelor party. Things are just kicking up. I don't want you at each other's throats all weekend."

"Me neither," I second the motion. "Especially if there will be casualties involved."

"Sorry. His swing is just so insulting." Rodney rakes his hands through his hair.

"Your fucking face is insulting," Landon mumbles under his breath, but we all hear him perfectly clear.

Telly breaks the tension with a loud belly laugh. "Stop playin' already. I want to finish this round. I'm kicking all your asses."

"We're letting you win," Rodney gripes.

"Sure, you are." Telly rolls his black eyes, the large square diamonds in his ears glinting in the sunlight. He gives it a second thought. "Maybe Kam is."

"Definitely not." I snort. I would never give up any kind of win. Ever.

I walk over to the golf cart to take a load off and grab some more ice. Fucking thing stings.

A minute later, Rodney joins me, leaving Landon and Telly to putt. Well, Telly is putting. Landon is stewing.

Rodney takes a seat behind the wheel and reaches back for a cold one. He cracks it open, takes a sip, then stares me down. What the fuck is his problem now?

"What?" I bite.

"Want to tell me what all that karma bullshit was about?"

"Huh?" I play dumb.

"That comment about you getting hit being karma. What the fuck is the universe pissed at you about?"

I roll my eyes and divert my attention away from him. I really don't want to get into this.

"Hey, I asked you a question." He nudges me.

"Are you wearing your asshole underwear today?"

"Don't I always?"

I turn my head to look at him. "Yes."

"So, want to tell me what's going through that thick noggin of yours?" He taps my head annoyingly, and I bat him away. "You've been acting weird lately."

"Just got shit on my mind."

"Is everything alright with Laney? The wedding?"

I nod. "Everything is fine with us . . . it's me . . ." I trail off.

"You?" he probes. "You having cold feet?"

"I have loser's remorse."

"What in the hell is that?" he questions before he realizes. "You feel guilty? Because we lost?"

I grit my teeth. "Because I'm the reason we lost." There, I said it. I'm the reason. I cost the entire team every second of their blood, sweat, and tears. Their time away from their family and all their faith in me. I'm the reason we lost it all.

"You really are an egomaniac," Rodney accuses.

"What the fuck is that supposed to mean?"

"It means we play football as a team. There is no one person who gets the blame when we win or lose."

"I threw a fucking interception. How am I not responsible?" I argue petulantly.

"Allen fumbled, twice. Brice missed a block, and you were sacked repeatedly. The way I see it, we all had a hand in that loss." He drains his beer then crushes the can against his forehead. I didn't think anyone over the age of seventeen did that, but then I met Rodney and was proven completely wrong.

"Hey, guys! Come get a load of this!" he shouts to Telly and Landon. "King QB thinks he's the sole reason we lost the Super Bowl."

I could kill him right now. Like literally split his skull open with a sand wedge and leave him on the green to die.

"Last time I ever confide in you," I mumble irritably.

"No, it's not. I'm about to fix your noggin."

"You like that word, don't you?" I ask, perturbed.

"My pop uses it. A lot," he admits.

"What are you two over here jabbering about?" Telly leans on his putter, Mr. Smooth and Cool.

"Kam thinks he's the reason we lost. He's carrying around 'it's all my fault' baggage. What a damn ego. Take all the glory for the wins and all the blame for the losses."

"Isn't that how it works? Quarterbacks, pitchers, centers. We are in the spotlight and get the gas and the fire."

"That is media bullshit. Team means together. No one person carries it all on their shoulders," Rodney reasons.

"I'm sorry, I don't see it that way."

"Then look at it like this. You led us to the big game. We're conference champs. Winning the Super Bowl just would have been gravy on top. But we are all proud," Telly chimes in. "We have the best QB in the league, and it's not just because you can throw a great pass. You're a great leader. A great role model. A great friend. Losing that game sucked, but there is no one else I want to play for. You lose, we all lose. You win, we all win. And do you know what will be even sweeter?"

"No, what?"

"Going back next year and dominating that title. What better story is there than a comeback? Than redemption? The way I see it, we're just set up to be legendary."

I stare quietly at Telly, Rodney, and Landon. My guilt has been eating me alive. "Do you all feel the same way?"

Landon and Rodney nod vigorously. "Life is freaking amazing. I've been in the NFL for one year, and I'm a conference champ, went to the Super Bowl, and have endorsements coming out of my ass. And you are a main contributor to that," Landon boasts. "One game doesn't define you," Rodney tacks on. "And maybe with all that extra money, you could hire a golf pro so you don't kill anyone on the course." He just has to throw a dig in at Landon. I swear it's compulsive.

"Are we straight, Q?" Telly puts his hand out. A little bit of pressure alleviates in my chest as he smiles at me. I clap his hand and smirk. For the first time in weeks, I don't feel so low, or tormented, or at fault.

"We're straight," I confirm.

"Good, 'cause we got some partyin' to do. It's my last weekend of freedom. We need to get CRAZY!" he bellows, doing his victory dance around the green. It's a booty shakin' strut with a signature helmet swipe.

Rodney and Landon join in, and now there are three massive football players owning hole four the same way they own the end zone. Something inside me breaks, and despite my neck still throbbing, I bust up with laughter. A deep, rumbling laugh that ends up being cathartic.

"C'mon, Q! Don't leave us hanging." Telly does this robotic dance walk thing toward me. I shake my head but stand. Then I let it all go with my boys. I pull out some old school dance moves, pump my pelvis, and do a little spin like nobody's watching.

I WON.

After our little victory dance on the golf course, I started to feel like my old self again. And with that came my confidence, cockiness, and desire to win. So, I did. By four strokes. Not bad for a guy who hasn't swung a club in months.

Landon has gotten nothing but hassled by the rest of the guys for nearly decapitating me. That story was priceless at dinner. My neck looks ugly though. It bruised bad and in the worst spot. Every time I move my head I'm reminded it's there.

Telly's bachelor party has lived up to expectations. Everyone is full, drunk, and currently being rubbed up on in a VIP lounge of a strip club. It's not really my scene, but it comes with the territory. I sip my beer and watch the shenanigans as time winds down.

Football players party hard, especially when given an excuse and in the off season. The liquor is flowing, testosterone is raging, and bills are raining. God, I can't even begin to think how much money is in those girl's G-strings.

"Dance, sugar?" a busty blonde offers me.

"I'm good." I tip my beer bottle. "Just watching."

"You sure? Maybe something a little more private is your speed?" she hisses in my ear.

"Nope, not my speed at all." I lightly push her away. "I'm good right where I am."

"Okay." She puckers her hot pink lips. "But if you change your mind, come find me. I'm Star."

"I'll remember that." Not. The only woman I'm interested in disappearing into a champagne room with is my fiancée.

I wonder if Laney would actually be up for that? I fantasize how killer she would look in a shiny G-string and nothing else. Under fluorescent lights giving me a lap dance.

Blood flows like a raging river to the head of my cock. Thank God I go home tomorrow.

I'm sure the last few weeks have been complete hell for Laney. I wasn't easy to deal with. I've been withdrawn, depressed and moody, but she never let her frustration show. She was just supportive. She gave me my space and was there when I needed her. I'm a total fucking dick. I was taking for granted all the great things I have in my life. I lost a football game. Not my career, or a friend, or a loved one.

I'm pretty damn blessed, and I lost sight of that for a minute.

Things are coming back into focus now, and I owe Laney something big. Some jewelry, a vacation, maybe I'll surprise her with a dream honeymoon. Tahiti is first on her wish list. Laney isn't one for expensive gifts. She likes simple things, but a woman as amazing as her, a woman who puts up with loving me and deals with the craziness of my life, deserves to get spoiled once in a while. And I have no problem spoiling her rotten.

"Yo, Q!" Landon yells with two girls on his arm. The rookie is having a good ol' time. "These ladies know a twenty-four-hour tattoo place! We're gonna go get ink. You in?" He sways on his feet a bit.

"Um . . ."

"C'mon, Ellis, don't be a pussy. Mark yourself already." Rodney goads me by flexing his sleeved arm. "Don't you want to look this good?"

I roll my eyes. "I look good, inked or not."

"Bet Laney would like it." Rodney hits me in my soft spot.

"Maybe," I ponder, draining my beer.

"So, let's go!" Landon howls, grabbing each of the girls' ass cheeks. He's on the road to a threesome, I call it right now.

We settle our tab while a few of the girls change before heading out of the club. It's like three a.m., and the effects of the alcohol are still going strong. When we walk out the front door, we're bombarded by camera flashes. Word must have gotten out about the pro football players partying it up. Shielding our faces and the girls from the paparazzi, we escape into the waiting limo.

Echoing laughs and giggles fill the stretch Lex as we pull away. One of the guy's sitting next to me rolls down the window to give the paparazzi the peace sign. Such an instigator.

We're packed in tight so the body heat index is high and the intoxication is brewing.

Rodney and Landon are completely captivated by their girls as we ride through town. Once we get to the shop, it looks like a clown car piling out. People just don't stop coming.

Inside the large parlor, neon lights glow, the sound of needles buzz, and the low hum of drunk athletes fills the space. The walls are covered with miles and miles of colorful art. Templates to choose from or ideas to gain inspiration.

Some of this stuff is really detailed.

"So, what are you thinking, Q?" Telly slaps me on the back. "Some tribal? Football number? Zodiac sign?" He snaps. "Passing record?"

All commendable recommendations, but none I'm interested in at the moment.

"I have something else in mind." I take a closer look at some text and smile.

LANEY

THE REGISTRY GUN BEEPS as I add a sterling silver platter to the wedding registry for Kam and me.

"Oh, nice choice," my mother compliments.

"I thought so. Dad's Thanksgiving turkey will look great on it." I laugh.

"Always thinking of others. That's my girl," she comments sarcastically as she squeezes me with one arm. Spending time with my mother these past few weeks has been beyond amazing. I can't remember the last time we spent more than seven consecutive days together. I'm getting too used to her being around, and the fact that she is so involved with helping me plan my wedding is completely spoiling me.

I wish she didn't have to travel so much. I wish she would put down roots, preferably close to where I live. But that is a pipe dream. My mother loves her job. She lives for it, much like Kam lives for his.

We peruse around Bloomingdale's, looking at household items to put on the registry. I'm half distracted thinking about my big presentation

Monday morning. I am finally revealing my designs to the partners at a business brunch. It's a risk because the building is so conservative, but I really think this added piece will work.

"Penny for your thoughts?" my mom asks as I stare off into space in front of a display of vases.

"Hmmm?" I snap out of my haze.

"You were daydreaming. Thinking about Kam?"

"Oh, no. Not at that moment. I was thinking about my meeting. I'm nervous," I confess as the glass dances with sparkles in front of us.

"Nervous about what? Presenting it?"

"If they are going to be receptive to the idea. If it's too out of the box for this project. You just never know. This design could make or break me in the firm."

"I have all the confidence in the world it's going to knock their socks off."

"We'll see."

"Don't doubt yourself, Laney. Confidence is the key to success."

"You would know. You're a rock star in business. It seems all the people I love are superheroes in their given field, and I'm just . . ." I shrug. "Normal. Average. Human."

"Laney," my mother's voice elevates as she turns me to look at her, "you are not average. You are amazing. You're strong, smart, funny. Do you think just anyone can love a man like Kam or a man like your father? No. And let me tell you a little secret. Superheroes need humans to strive. You're what gives us our power." She takes my face, her blue eyes full of love and compassion. "You are still so young. You have so much to learn and such an incredible career ahead of you. Even if the partners don't go for the idea, they will respect your initiative, and you will stand out to them for your creativity. Trust me, I know. A smart professional who shows promise makes an impact. Believe in yourself. I do. I always have. Even when you were five and you told me you wanted to fly helicopters, I believed you could do it."

"That's still on my bucket list," I divulge.

"That doesn't surprise me. Please, promise me you won't compare yourself. Just be you. It's why we all love you." She kisses my forehead. I nod.

"Good. Now let's go look at luggage for the out-of-this-world honeymoon I'm going to send you on."

"Mom." I grab her arm. "You don't have to do that."

"I know. But you are my only daughter, and I want to. Besides, who better than me to plan a trip? I know all the good spots," she whispers conspiratorially.

"Can it be someplace tropical?"

"Definitely." She drags me through the store. Just as we get into kitchenware, I stop short.

"Oh, my God." I hurry to a mannequin wearing an apron. It's pink, frilly, obnoxiously sparkly, and proclaims "Queen of the Kitchen, Bitch" proudly across the top. In fuchsia lettering, no less.

"Laney, really?"

"It's perfect."

"For whom?"

"Kam."

"'Scuse me?"

"It's a joke. I have to get it."

My mother curls her lip in gaudy disgust. "If you must."

"I must."

I PICK UP KAM'S present from the kitchen counter. I had it wrapped in shiny silver paper. I tried to call him before bed last night, but his phone went straight to voicemail. I know what happens when he goes out with his teammates. Mayhem, but he at least usually sends me a goodnight text. I will make sure to give him plenty of shit for ignoring me when he gets home.

I smile to myself. Kam has always made it way too easy.

I'm supposed to be meeting my mother for breakfast so I won't be here when Kam gets home. I'm saving this baby for later. I can't wait to see his face. Hopefully it makes him laugh. I miss hearing Kam laugh. I miss seeing his easy smile.

I pray this weekend did him some good.

Finishing the last of my coffee, I hear something that catches my attention during the celebrity gossip portion of the weekend news.

"A few New York elite were caught partying it up last night at a popular strip club right outside Myrtle Beach," the newscaster in plaid excitedly exaggerates. I spy on the television screen close to a dozen familiar faces escaping out the front door of the club with a few girls mixed in. One face gains my full attention as the broadcast goes on. "It seems New York's golden boy didn't miss out on any of the fun. Wonder what the future Mrs. Ellis will think?" the man mocks as the video freezes on an image of Kam in the limo window with an obnoxious red arrow pointing at his neck. It feels like I've been slapped in the face in front of the whole northeast. Kam smiling with a gigantic hickey displayed proudly on his neck. Rage ignites inside me like I've never felt before.

When I told Kam to go blow off some steam, I didn't mean with a fucking stripper.

KAM

I CAN'T WAIT TO see Laney. She's all I could think about on the plane ride home. I concocted a huge plan to take her out to her favorite restaurant tonight, shower her with compliments and affection, and let her pick out whatever she wants at the closed jewelry store. She deserves at least that. And then when we get home, I'm going to make love to her while she's wearing that piece of jewelry and nothing else.

My blood is pumping already. I haven't felt this good in weeks.

"Lemon!" I burst through the front door of our condo, ready to tackle Laney, but I'm met with a surprise instead.

"Asshole!" I duck just as my prize, signed football comes careening toward my head. It misses me by half an inch and shatters the window behind me.

What the flying fuck?

"How could you!" Laney verbally pounces on me as I collect my bearings. What the fuck is going on?

"How could I what?" I put my hands up and take a step back as she charges.

"Don't fucking play dumb. It's all over the news. You and your good time last night! Jesus, Kam, if you were going to cheat on me, could you have at least been discreet about it? Did you have to flaunt it in my face and make me look like a goddamn jackass?" she unloads, and I'm left speechless.

"I didn't—"

"Don't. Don't you dare," she cuts me off. I have never seen her so livid. "I have done nothing but try and be the doting fiancée the past few weeks. Tried to give you everything you need. Space, time, understanding, love, and this is what I get? A public slap in the face? I know you're upset, and I know you are hurting. But I don't even know who you are right now." She rips off her engagement ring, and I choke. Her focus is zeroed in on my neck, and it's then I realize what she thinks.

"This isn't a hickey."

"Oh, please." She chucks the ring at me and I barely catch it. "Don't insult my fucking intelligence. I saw you come out of the strip club with all those girls. It looks like one of them latched on to you like a suction cup. Did you let her suck your fucking blood like a vampire? That damn thing is huge." She pushes past me, and I grab her arm, desperate for her to calm down and just listen.

"Goddammit, Laney."

"Don't fucking touch me." She jerks away, anger raging in her big blue, watery eyes. For a split-second, things are calm, silent. Laney shakes her head at me with shame before she escapes out the front door. I'm at a loss what to do. Should I chase her? Give her some space and let her calm down? My decision to go after her is too little too late, because just as I make it out the door, she speeds off in the silver Audi I bought her for her birthday.

I slump on the sidewalk eating her dust.

Shit just got really fucked up.

Chapter Ten

LANEY

I POUND ON MY mother's hotel room door.

I kept it together the whole way here, but as soon as she answers and I see her confused face, I break down in tears.

"Oh, honey. What happened?" she asks as I fall into her arms.

"Kam and his big fat hickey happened," I blubber. My mother walks me inside the suite and places me down on the living room sofa. The room is modern and spacious and full of natural light from the large windows, but all I see is gray. She hands me a wad of tissues and places a glass of water on the table as I cry it all out. I feel so . . . stupid. And betrayed and let down. I always believed in Kam, even when we weren't together, but if this is what life is going to be like. If his highs and lows spin him out of control and he makes destructive decisions like this, our future is over before it even began. I wipe my wet face with the tissues and take a big gulp of water.

"Can you tell me what happened now?" My mother sits next to me. Her hair is in a bun, she has no makeup on, and she's still in sweats. It's a form you very rarely see my mother in. Usually she's all class all the time.

"Kam cheated on me in front of the whole world." I'm completely humiliated.

She gives me a strange look. "Kam cheated?"

"Yes." I sniff. "Why is that so hard to believe?"

"Because it's Kam."

"What is that supposed to mean?"

"Honey." My mother shifts me so we are face to face. I can barely look at her. "I have known a lot of men in my life. Good ones, great ones, terrible ones, and I can tell you Kam is one of the best. He's head over heels in love with you. I can't believe he cheated on you."

"You're taking his side?" I ask, aghast.

"No. I'm not taking anyone's side. I just find it very hard to believe."

"He has a hickey the size of Jupiter on his neck. Evidence."

"Well, that I can't explain. But did you at least hear what he had to say? Did he admit to cheating on you?"

"It was splashed all over TV." I erupt. "What more proof do I need?"

"Did you hear him out, or did you just react?"

"I reacted," I admit. But I saw it with my own eyes. He was at a strip club, leaving with girls. His eyes were bloodshot, and the hickey. "You have no idea what it's like to love a celebrity." Living with constant ridicule, under a microscope. You sneeze, and someone tweets about it. It's pressure all the damn time.

"I don't?" She snorts. "Cold-hearted business bitch leaves lovable Chef Riley," she quotes. "Your father and I were over long before he became a household name, but I still caught the heat when we divorced. I understand, baby. I do."

I forgot my parents were still sort of together when my dad's career started to really take off. Technically, they were still married, but my mom traveled so much it was like they were living apart.

I drop my head in my hands at a loss.

My phone rings in my pocket, again. It's been doing that a lot. It's

Kam. I've ignored every call. Pulling the phone out, I hand it to my mother. "Can you flush this down the toilet?" She straightens, taking the phone robotically. She ignores the call and then stands. "I have a much better idea." I watch as she walks in and then out of the bathroom, before shutting the door. "I didn't flush it, but I did hide it," she informs me as she opens the mini fridge and pulls out a bottle of champagne and a small container of orange juice. "Mimosas make everything better." She pops the champagne cork. The mouth of the bottle smokes a bit. My mother mixes two drinks, both heavy on the bubbly, then plops down beside me. I take the glass more than willingly.

For the next several hours, we binge watch bad TV, eat all the bad things, and polish off two more bottles of champagne.

I'm still completely miserable, but being with my mom somehow makes the pain bearable.

"Mom," I mutter against her shoulder.

"Mmm?"

"Thanks."

She kisses my head. "It's what I'm here for."

"I sort of wish you were here all the time." I know I shouldn't have said that, but it's the truth. Spending these last few weeks with my mom, basically having her on demand, has made me realize how much I love having her in my life.

"What if I was?" she fishes. I raise my head off her shoulder.

"What if you were, what?"

"I was going to talk to you at breakfast, but then the world ended, so I thought it would be better discussed at a later time."

"What would be?" I push.

"Me, staying in New York permanently."

"Really? No more traveling?" I perk up.

"Very little. The company wants to stand up a new international office in midtown. They want to bring the clientele here, to the US, and have asked me repeatedly to run it. I've always said no, but being here with you, helping you plan your wedding, seeing how much I've missed." She shrugs. "I was thinking maybe it's time to hang up my suitcase for a while."

My eyes water for the umpteenth time today. "I think I would love that."

Is it possible to lose someone you love and gain someone you love all in one day? I'm not sure how much more my heart can take. Right now, it's being held together with duct tape.

"I don't know what to do about Kam," I confess. "I have to go home, but I don't want to see him." I've been fretting about this all day. "My presentation is tomorrow. I need clothes." Luckily my portfolio is in the office. "I can't show up in jeans." I know if I go home, World War III will break out, and I just can't afford to be emotionally shipwrecked right now. I need to keep it together, at least until after the presentation. My relationship can fall to shit after that. Not that I want it to.

At all.

Kam and I worked so hard to build this life, I don't understand why he would just throw it all away.

The thought of him with another woman makes my stomach hurt. It's exactly the same feeling I got when I saw him come out of the storage closet with Darcy in high school. He was innocent then, maybe he's innocent now? Maybe there's a logical explanation? Maybe I've lost half my damn mind? He has a hickey. The evidence is there. I can't stop myself from wondering how many other women he's been with, and I can't get Monique's voice out of my head. "Everything is all wonderful in the beginning." Her French accent drips with disdain. "You have kids, a beautiful home, the American dream, so you say. Then you find out it's all a ruse. A scam, because your wonderful husband has been cheating on you the whole time. You are the fool and everyone knew it but you."

"Well, you know the great thing about having a power CEO for a mother?" My mom gets up off the couch and drags me with her. All the way into the bedroom. "Her wardrobe." She opens her closet. It's stuffed with all kinds of amazing clothes. She grabs a hanger and pulls out a suit. "This is my favorite. Always brings me luck, and it looks just about your size." She smiles as she holds up the black Versace jumpsuit to my body.

"In this outfit, you can run the world." The corporate shark circles and flails.

"I don't feel like I could run around the block right now."

"You will. You're my daughter. All you know is how to survive. I couldn't be prouder of the woman you've become. I wish I could take more credit for it."

"I give you plenty of credit." I hug her. "Even though you weren't there, you always knew what to say."

"I'm glad I did one thing right." Hearing my mom divulge insecurities is somewhat odd. She barely ever shows weakness, but ever since she came back into town, she's been different. More maternal, softer, approachable. I like this side of her. I like that she can be strong and soft all at the same time. It's exactly how I want to be.

"Do you know what would make you the best mom in the world?"

"No, what?"

"If you'd let me have chocolate cake for dinner."

She sighs dramatically. "Just this once. And I know the perfect place to order from."

KAM BLEW UP MY phone all night. And all morning. I can't talk to him right now. I'm too nervous to think about anything but this meeting, and the slightest distraction will no doubt throw me off my game. I want to impress my bosses, not dissolve into an emotional mess because I had a fight with my fiancé. I want to be able to block it all out and get shit done.

Sitting at a rectangular table by the front window in a trendy little restaurant in midtown I nervously present my idea to Tom and Joe, the owners of the company, and my bosses. They're a gay power couple who have a sharp eye for design and forward way of thinking when it comes to business. It's part of the reason I wanted to work for them so badly. Their buildings and décor spoke to me on so many levels. They inspired me while studying at college, and when I applied for an internship, I never in a million years thought I would get it. But I did.

Tom and Joe sit causally across from me in designer suits sipping espresso as I show them the AutoCAD design for the entryway and lobby.

"I know the building has a very conservative feel, but I think if we incorporated a water feature and cascading florals, it will complement the high-end aspect and add a welcoming feel."

I show them the placement of the three-story water wall and bright climbing florals that will grow naturally on each side. The building has an abundance of natural light, so the water will sparkle and the plants will thrive.

Tom and Joe both nod their heads as I speak, but their attention is distracted. They keep looking over my shoulder. It's nerve-wracking as hell. It feels like my attempts are failing. I want to panic, but I don't. I just keep going, hoping I say something that will spark their interest. That doesn't look like it's happening, though.

Tom puts his cup down, and it clanks on the small saucer. "Is that Martel Lewis, Rodney Pines, and Landon Knobs signing autographs outside?" He asks, perplexed. I whip my head around to find a small crowd gathering outside the restaurant as all three of them sign autographs. What in the hell?

When Landon spots me spying, he slides over to the glass and taps on it, beckoning me outside. I'm sure I turn white. The biggest business meeting of my short career and it's being crashed by three of Kam's teammates. If he put them up to this, I swear . . .

I turn back to my bosses and smile uncomfortably. I decide to ignore the spectacle outside. I'll deal with it later, but it turns out, pretending it's not there is easier said than done.

There's another tap on the window, and then a muted "Laney! We need to talk to you."

That embarrassed smile is plastered to my face. This is a fucking nightmare.

"Maybe you should see what they want, Laney," Tom suggests. I glance back; the crowd is getting bigger and my frustration is growing just as fast.

"Maybe I should. I am terribly sorry, I'll just be a minute." I hope.

I speed walk through the restaurant in the four-inch heels my mom let me borrow. I wonder if anything like this has ever happened at one of her business meetings? Probably not.

I burst out the front door into the chilly February morning, grateful the jumpsuit came with a matching blazer.

"What in the hell are the three of you doing here?" There is a fake smile on my face and real pissed off tone in my voice.

"Laney, we need to talk to you," Telly informs me.

"Right now? While I'm with my bosses?" All four of us look through the window. Tom and Joe are watching our every move. Rodney smiles and waves, and they both return the gesture. I want to scream.

"Look, we really needed to talk to you." Telly puts his arm around me and starts walking down the street.

"Hey, guys! We'll finish autographs in just a sec, but we need to talk to this pretty lady first!" Rodney voices from behind me. A police officer approaches just as we make it to the corner. "Officer, a little help, please," Telly requests. "We're not trying to cause a traffic jam, but we do need to have an important conversation in private." The officer nods with understanding, and I hear him announce something to the following crowd as the four of us duck into a hotel lobby. Inside, there are several different hallways leading to street exits. They seem to know exactly where they're going because they steer me down one that is tucked away and empty.

"Been here before?" I ask briskly.

"Couple times. You can book by the hour." Rodney provides way too much information.

Someone, please, save me.

"What do you guys want?" I cut right to the chase. "Did Kam send you?" Because I'm gonna kill him.

"No, he didn't send us, but he did tell us what happened. And we want to set the record straight," Telly explains.

"There's nothing to set straight. Kam cheated on me. It's all over social media. At your bachelor party." I shoot laser beams at him.

"That's just it. He didn't," Telly immediately shoots back, as if I'd believe him.

"Of course, you're going to say that. You're his boys. You would do anything for him," I argue adamantly.

"That's exactly right," Rodney jumps in, realizing just how self-incriminating that statement was. "What I mean is, yes, we would do anything for him, and that's why we're here. Not to cover anything up. To uncover the truth." He is very proud of his backpedaling.

"What the hell are you talking about?" My patience is running thin. I'm stressed, I'm tired, and I'm heartbroken. I just want to go back to my mom's and drown myself in a gallon of ice cream. The last thing I need are these jokers making my life more complicated.

"Kam didn't cheat. Yes, we went to a strip club Saturday night, and yes, some of the guys went home with a girl."

"Or two girls," Landon adds.

Dear Lord.

Telly fires a death stare at Landon before he continues. "Regardless of how many girls the other guys went home with, Kam had zero interest in any of them. He sat in the corner all night just sipping on beer. No lap dances, no nothing."

I cross my arms and glare at Telly. Does he think I am a complete idiot? "Telly, there is a hickey the size of a black hole on Kam's neck. Do you honestly expect me to believe that bullshit story?"

"Yes!" all three of them answer, andI lean back warily.

"We expect you to believe it, because it's the truth. Kam doesn't know we're here, and he'd probably kill us if he found out, but we wanted to tell you in person that it's all Landon's fault." Rodney throws Landon right under the bus.

"Hey, if you didn't ride my ass during golf, I wouldn't have gotten so pissed off and almost decapitated Kam. So, if it's anyone's fault, it's yours."

"'Scuse me? Did you just say you almost decapitated my fiancé?"

"Yes!" Telly throws up his hands animatedly. "This is what we are trying to tell you. That hickey on Kam's neck you think came from a stripper really came from a sixty-mile-an-hour golf ball."

I have heard it all. I stare Telly down. "How long did it take the three of you to come up with that lame story?"

"It's not a story." Rodney pulls out his phone. "Look, I have a timeline." He starts scrolling through pictures. "Here's one on the plane. No hickey. And here is us at dinner Friday night, no hickey. And here is us in the hotel room early Saturday morning before golf." That picture is a close-up of Kam lying on the bed, his neck clearly visible, and also someone's naked ass cheeks.

"I never need to see that picture again." I close my eyes. What is it about athletes and their free-range nakedness?

"Okay, and here we are on hole one and, look, then again on hole four right after Landon tried to decapitate Kam."

Kam is sitting on the back of a golf cart with a perturbed look on his face and a handful of ice to his neck. The next picture is the real evidence. A shot of Kam's bruised neck. The exact place the incriminating hickey is.

"Look." Rodney enlarges the picture. "You can even see the golf ball divots in his skin."

"Oh, shit." My stomach drops as I inspect the image.

"Laney, Kam would never, ever cheat on you. There are a lot of dogs in the league, but Kam is not one of them. He is disgustingly crazy about you. I can't tell you how many times the guys talk about some honey, bragging about how gorgeous she is, and Kam always says no one is as beautiful as his Lemon. No one is as funny, or sexy, or smart, or strong, or . . ."

"Okay, I got it," I cut Rodney off. "I'm perfect."

"Kam definitely thinks so." Telly puts his hands on my shoulders. "Chris and I have gone through the exact same thing. The media likes to stir the pot. You can't believe everything they report."

"Most of what they report." Rodney snorts.

"I usually don't. I trust Kam. But when I saw physical evidence I sort of lost it."

"We understand. We know how it rolls." Telly smiles. His dark eyes are as warm as his sentiment. "This life isn't easy, and when you find a solid person to be with, you don't fuck it up."

"Speaking from experience?"

"You know it." The large diamond studs in his ears wink at me under the fluorescent lights.

"I guess I should call him back, huh?"

"I would go see in him in person. He's torn up," Telly advises. Shit.

"He's that bad?" I bite my lip.

"Oh, yeah," he breathes out. "'Bout as bad as a catastrophic disaster."

AFTER PROFUSELY APOLOGIZING TO my bosses, I made amends for the botched breakfast by letting them finish the meal with Landon, Telly, and Rodney. Tom and Joe were loving life when I left. Sometimes knowing people in high places can really help you save face.

I rush up the front stairs to our condo and barrel inside just to run smack dab into Kam in the foyer. We literally collide. He grabs me just before I fall flat on my ass and an awkward moment passes.

"Laney!"

"Hi." I look up at him as I dangle in his arms. He pulls me into a hug and buries his face in my neck. I dissolve. All the pain and anguish and hurt melts away as Kam holds me tight.

"I didn't know if you were coming back," he mumbles against my skin.

"I wasn't going to, but you have some really, really loyal teammates and friends." Kam separates us just enough so he can look into my eyes. His are glassy and bloodshot and rimmed with dark circles. I don't think he slept a wink last night. I provide an answer to his questioning expression. "Telly, Landon, and Rodney crashed my business breakfast this morning." Horror mars his handsome face.

"They did what?"

"Don't freak out. I handled that for both of us." I place my hands on his hard chest. "They showed up, made a spectacle in front of the restaurant, accidentally of course, then demanded I hear them out. So, I did."

"They told you what happened? On the golf course?"

"Yes, and at dinner, and the strip club. I saw plenty of pictures." I roll my eyes.

"So, you know I didn't cheat. Laney, I would never do that. It's not who I am. I love you. I've loved you since the moment you sat down next to me in chemistry class senior year. This may sound crazy, but after that class, I knew you were the girl I was going to marry."

"It does sound crazy, but I know it's true. I'm sorry I freaked out. I was feeling so much pressure with the presentation and the wedding and you being so depressed, I think I just sort of snapped. I should have heard you out. I'm sorry." I lift up onto my toes to kiss him. He accepts my lips willingly, kissing me like a desperate man, suffocating from a lack of oxygen.

"Don't be sorry, just never leave me again," he proclaims between kisses. "You're mine, Laney, and I'm yours. Don't ever doubt that. No one will ever be you, and nothing or nobody will ever come between us. You're my foundation, and I need you. I love you."

"I need you, too."

"What about love me?"

"That goes without saying. I gave you my heart when I was eighteen, and I never got it back."

"That's because it's mine. All mine."

"You know what else is yours?"

"What?" he answers in a hoarse whisper. The sound travels down my spine like an electric current.

I pull off my jacket and the blazer underneath, showing off the formfitting black jumper. Kam's eyes widen and his lips part. He scans the halter top, dragging his eyes over my bare shoulders, my modest cleavage from the plunging neckline, the pinched waist, loose material over my legs and the strappy four inch heels that are to die for.

"Where?" He clears his throat. "Where did you get that outfit from?"

"You like?"

He nods vigorously.

"My mom has an awesome wardrobe."

"Fuck yeah, she does," Kam agrees as he slides his hands around my waist and then down to my bottom. "I missed this ass, and these lips, and those eyes, and that smile." He nips at me.

"Oh, yeah? Take me to bed and show me how much."

"Done." He chews on my neck, causing me to squirm and giggle. "Kam, you're going to give me a hickey!"

"I know. I want you to have one that matches mine." He bites down hard, and I squeal. "Kam!"

He laughs darkly before letting me go and grabs my hand. Hurrying me into our bedroom, he sits me down on the bed then disappears into his closet.

"What are you doing?"

"Getting this." He reappears, walks straight over to me, and drops to one knee. "Never take this ring off your finger again. Right here is where it belongs." He slips the white gold band with magnificent diamond back onto my finger.

I admire it. "Yes, that's definitely where it belongs. And I definitely belong with you."

"Damn right, you do. Completely naked." Kam attacks the clasp at the nape of my neck. He unfastens it in a nanosecond, causing the material to fall to my waist, exposing my bare breasts.

"Fuck, no bra," he groans, tormented.

"No bra," I confirm, and he smashes his mouth to mine, massaging both my breasts. We get swept away in the passionate moment, reconnecting, rebuilding, reforging the pathway back to us. Clothes are ripped from our bodies and thrown onto the floor without a second thought. There's nothing left between us. No reservations or doubts or insecurities. We're where we're meant to be. With each other.

Kam runs his tongue all along my body, over my shoulders, between my heaving breasts, down the center of my torso, nibbling my hip bones until he rests right between my thighs. There's no hesitation, no second thought, he just spreads my legs and claims what's his. Eating me out with the force of a raging river. I writhe on the bed, my legs wrapped around his head, my hands cemented to his hair.

He swirls his tongue up then down, covering every inch of my slit several times over, stabbing into my entrance when I least expect, and latching onto my clit to close the deal. He sucks with the perfect amount of pressure to make me see stars, and when he sinks his finger inside me, delivering the final blow, I explode. My entire body shakes and my moans hit octaves I wasn't aware my voice was capable of. Kam just continues to lick and finger me through the tremors, until my body can't take any more and just gives out.

I lie limp on the bed, panting in my blissed-out state as Kam climbs up my body. He's all power, raw and animalistic, raging to come.

I spread my legs, beckoning him inside me. This is what I want, what I need. Kam to take me, to own me, to love me. With a powerful thrust, he drives into me, and we both cry out. He's harder than a rock and hungrier than a lion. My body responds, soaking his surging cock with excitement. With arousal.

"Fuck, Kam," I can barely breathe as we both rock our hips as hard and fast as we can.

"Laney, it's only you. It will only ever be you," he pants, as he picks up the pace, the stroke of his cock becoming deeper and more aggressive.

We're both gasping for air within a few seconds, the moment of impact pending.

"Kam, you're going to make me come again." My limbs lock up as his pelvis grazes my clit and his swollen erection fills me to the brim.

"That's what I want. You to come all over me. All fucking over me." The muscles on his back are as rigid as a mountain range as we fuck. My hair is matted from sweat, and my thighs are sore from all the physical tension, but it's my core that traps me in the moment. Because when it finally catches fire, it burns me alive. I feel the orgasm everywhere, from the tips of my toes to the ends of my hair.

I latch onto Kam, spewing every curse word in the book as I come freely and gloriously. All my cells pulse, my eyelids flutter, and my pussy aches as he climaxes mere seconds after me.

We're imprisoned within each other, and it's a life sentence I will gladly live out. Because with Kam I can do anything and be anyone. He said I was his foundation, he's definitely mine, too.

I felt it the first time he kissed me all those years ago. Before I met him, my feet were dangling, and after I met him, they were planted firmly on the ground.

"I love you, Laney," he groans, high on ecstasy.

"I love you, too." I touch his face, spent, satisfied, and spoken for by the boy who demanded my heart and the man who vows to keep it safe.

Keep it forever.

We lie lazily soaking up the reconnection. "Does it hurt?" I touch the angry bruise on Kam's neck.

"Only when someone pokes it." He grits his teeth. I laugh apologetically.

"Sorry."

"It's fine." He tightens his arm around me and closes his eyes.

"You had a pretty rough weekend, huh? Almost getting decapitated twice? What do you think the odds of that are?" I ponder.

"A zillion to one, I'm sure."

"Well, the odds have always been in your favor."

"Lucky me."

"Yes, lucky you." I pinch him.

"Ouch! What was that for?"

"Just making sure you know how lucky you are."

"I know. Trust me, I know. I was an emotional wreck there for a while. And I'm sorry."

I lift my head, my dark hair falling over my shoulder like a veil. "You don't have to be sorry. I know you carry around a lot of responsibility. And I know you care about your team like they're a litter of puppies."

"They definitely feel like a litter of puppies sometimes." He snorts.

"My point is, what makes you so amazing is that you care so much. And I get it. I understand you."

"I know you do. You always have." Kam laces our fingers together and flashes my diamond in the rays of sunlight streaking through the wall of windows. Tiny rainbows dance on the surface. "Which is why I got this while I was away." He shows me his wrist. It's covered with a small bandage. I was so caught up in the makeup frenzy, I was completely oblivious to it.

"What did you do?" I perk up.

"Something that felt totally right. Peel it off."

I do as he asks, detaching the tape gently while eager to see what's underneath. Cursive writing comes into view with a small lemon on a branch strategically placed off to the side.

"Oh, my God, Kam. A tattoo?"

"Yup," he states proudly. "Do you like?"

The inscription reads "Better than I was. More than I am."

I freakin' disintegrate. "I love." I pout.

"You love? Then what's that face for?"

"Because I want a matching one. With a football, of course."

Kam beams. "I'm sure we can arrange that." He pulls me into his body and hugs me tightly. Our limbs tangled and skin warm.

This, right here, is the heart of everything. Of us. No spotlights, or reporters, or screaming fans. Just a simple southern boy and the sassy city girl he loves. The sassy city girl who loves him back. Who understands the myth, the man, the legend, and knows exactly who the true person is inside.

EPILOGUE

KAM

I'M SO NERVOUS MY hands are sweating and my collar is choking me.

I look out into the large crowd of our closest family and friends, and I wonder if they can pick up on my unease. I'm used to performing under pressure, but standing on this altar waiting for Laney to appear is the most nerve-wracking moment of my life. Big game pressure doesn't hold a candle to your wedding day.

Just when I think I can't take another second of waiting, the processional music begins. My stomach does somersaults as one by one Laney's bridesmaids walk slowly down the long white runner dressed in dark purple carrying multicolored bouquets. The last six months have been a hurricane. Pulling this wedding together in such a short amount of time proved to be a monumental undertaking considering the size. But we did it. We worked together and pulled it off, and now here we are.

It's how we do things. We're a team.

In reality, she's the quarterback and I'm her center. Here to protect her. And I plan to do just that, for the rest of our lives.

The music suddenly changes to the wedding march, and all of our guests stand up. I'm so anxious I'm about to jump right out of my tux.

But when I see Laney suddenly appear, I feel nothing but calm. Everything just seems to fall into place. And despite being surrounded by the most magnificent gardens I have ever seen, nature's beauty doesn't compare to the woman walking toward me. The woman who believed in me when I didn't, supported me when I felt most alone, and stood by me in my darkest hour.

I drink in every inch of her, wanting to commit this moment to memory—every detail of her dress, the way the sparkles of her bodice shine, the way the form-fitting material clings to her curves, and how the flair below her knees kicks up slightly with every step closer to me. But it's the look on her face that will be ingrained in me forever. The slight, shy smile, a contrast to the excitement in her big blue eyes. That's all for me. It's all mine.

"Who gives this woman away?" the minister asks once Laney finally reaches us.

"I do," Riley, her father, proudly announces as he hands her off to me. I'm speechless, barely able to breathe as she stands before me.

"Kam, are you okay?" Laney whispers. I've suddenly forgotten how to form sentences. A few silent moments pass before the minster chimes in. "I believe, my dear, you have taken his breath away."

I nod. Yes, that. Totally, that.

Laney's smile is blinding. "I guess you like the dress."

"I love it. And you." I lean in to kiss her without even thinking and the minister puts the kibosh on it with his hand.

"Save it for the end. I promise the wait will be worth it." He winks, and the guests sitting in the front row laugh.

"The wait has been worth it." Laney bares all, her eyes glassy with tears.

It sure as hell has, and all I can think, as the sun sets, turning the sky pink, is this is the most perfect twilight of my life.

I hope you enjoyed the Southern Nights series! Interested in knowing more about my works? Visit *www.mneverauthor.com* Dark romance your thing? Check out the Decadence After Dark series! I also have two contemporary ménage standalones waiting for you. Bad boy bikers? Grab *Moto*! Two seductive strangers? Shane and Chase are waiting to seduce you in *Trinity*. How about a hot romantic suspense? Ghostface Killer it is! Don't forget to sign up for my newsletter and join my readers group for a ton of naughty fun! Books, boys, and giveaways!

The Naughty List (M. Never's newsletter)
M. Never's Naughty Reader Group on Facebook

ABOUT THE AUTHOR

M. NEVER RESIDES IN NEW York City. When she's not researching ways to tie up her characters in compromising positions, you can usually find her at the gym kicking the crap out of a punching bag, or eating at some trendy new restaurant.

    She has a dependence on sushi, a fetish for boots, and is stalked by a clingy pit bull named Apache. She is surrounded by family and friends she wouldn't trade for the world and is a little in love with her readers. The more the merrier. So make sure to say hi!

www.mneverauthor.com
#ProvocativeRomance

BOOKS BY M. NEVER

Owned (Decadence After Dark Book 1)
Claimed (Decadence After Dark Book 2)
Ruined (A Decadence After Dark Epilogue)
The Decadence After Dark Box Set (Books 1–3)
Lie With Me (Decadence After Dark Book 4)
Elicit (Decadence After Dark Book 5)

Moto: A MFM Ménage Romance

Trinity: A MMF Ménage Romance

Ghostface Killer

www.mneverauthor.com
#ProvocativeRomance

ACKNOWLEDGEMENTS

MY BIGGEST THANKS GOES to the army who supports me. My editor, proofreaders and formatter are so understanding and willing to work with all my craziness. Without their patience, I don't know what I would do!

To my PAs Sarah and Melissa and my PR Linda Russel, thank you for being my rocks and being there for whatever I need. You keep me sane!

To the bloggers and the readers. Thank you so much for wanting this book. You're the foundation. I write for myself and then share it with all of you. Thank you for coming into my world and allowing me into yours!

Until the next!

Made in United States
North Haven, CT
11 October 2023

42631474R00136